James Whitcomb Riley

Green fields and running Brooks

James Whitcomb Riley

Green fields and running Brooks

ISBN/EAN: 9783743356900

Manufactured in Europe, USA, Canada, Australia, Japa

Cover: Foto ©Andreas Hilbeck / pixelio.de

Manufactured and distributed by brebook publishing software (www.brebook.com)

James Whitcomb Riley

Green fields and running Brooks

GREEN FIELDS AND RUNNING BROOKS

JAMES WHITCOMB RILEY

INDIANAPOLIS
THE BOBBS-MERRILL COMPANY
PUBLISHERS

PRESS OF
BRAUNWORTH & CO.
BOOKBINDERS AND PRINTERS
BROOKLYN, N. Y.

TO MY SISTERS

ELVA AND MARY

CONTENTS.

(7)

GREEN FIELDS AND

RUNNING BROOKS

(11)

HO! green fields and running brooks!
  Knotted strings and fishing-hooks
Of the truant, stealing down
Weedy backways of the town.

  Where the sunshine overlooks,
  By green fields and running brooks,
  All intruding guests of chance
  With a golden tolerance.

Cooing doves, or pensive pair
Of picnickers, straying there—
By green fields and running brooks,
Sylvan shades and mossy nooks!

  And—O Dreamer of the Days,
  Murmurer of roundelays
  All unsung of words or books,
  Sing green fields and running brooks!

A COUNTRY PATHWAY.

I COME upon it suddenly, alone—
  A little pathway winding in the weeds
That fringe the roadside ; and with dreams my own,
  I wander as it leads.

Full wistfully along the slender way,
  Through summer tan of freckled shade and shine,
I take the path that leads me as it may—
  Its every choice is mine.

A chipmunk, or a sudden-whirring quail,
  Is startled by my step as on I fare—
A garter-snake across the dusty trail
  Glances and–is not there.

Above the arching jimson-weeds flare twos
  And twos of sallow-yellow butterflies,
Like blooms of lorn primroses blowing loose
  When autumn winds arise.

The trail dips—dwindles—broadens then, and lifts
  Itself astride a cross-road dubiously,
And, from the fennel marge beyond it, drifts
  Still onward, beckoning me.

And though it needs must lure me mile on mile
  Out of the public highway, still I go,
My thoughts, far in advance in Indian-file,
  Allure me even so.

Why, I am as a long-lost boy that went
  At dusk to bring the cattle to the bars,
And was not found again, though Heaven lent
  His mother all the stars

With which to seek him through that awful night.
  O years of nights as vain!—Stars never rise
But well might miss their glitter in the light
  Of tears in mother-eyes!

So—on, with quickened breaths, I follow still—
  My *avant-courier* must be obeyed!
Thus am I led, and thus the path, at will,
  Invites me to invade

A meadow's precincts, where my daring guide
  Clambers the steps of an old-fashioned stile,
And stumbles down again, the other side,
  To gambol there awhile

In pranks of hide-and-seek, as on ahead
  I see it running, while the clover-stalks
Shake rosy fists at me, as though they said—
  "You dog our country-walks

"And mutilate us with your walking-stick!—
   We will not suffer tamely what you do
And warn you at your peril,—for we 'll sic
   Our bumble-bees on you!"

But I smile back, in airy nonchalance,—
   The more determined on my wayward quest,
As some bright memory a moment dawns
   A morning in my breast—

Sending a thrill that hurries me along
   In faulty similes of childish skips,
Enthused with lithe contortions of a song
   Performing on my lips.

In wild meanderings o'er pasture wealth—
   Erratic wanderings through dead'ning-lands,
Where sly old brambles, plucking me by stealth,
   Put berries in my hands:

Or, the path climbs a boulder—wades a slough—
   Or, rollicking through buttercups and flags,
Goes gaily dancing o'er a deep bayou
   On old tree-trunks and snags:

Or, at the creek, leads o'er a limpid pool
   Upon a bridge the stream itself has made,
With some Spring-freshet for the mighty tool
   That its foundation laid.

I pause a moment here to bend and muse,
  With dreamy eyes, on my reflection, where
A boat-backed bug drifts on a helpless cruise,
  Or wildly oars the air,

As, dimly seen, the pirate of the brook—
  The pike, whose jaunty hulk denotes his speed—
Swings pivoting about, with wary look
  Of low and cunning greed.

Till, filled with other thought, I turn again
  To where the pathway enters in a realm
Of lordly woodland, under sovereign reign
  Of towering oak and elm.

A puritanic quiet here reviles
  The almost whispered warble from the hedge,
And takes a locust's rasping voice and files
  The silence to an edge.

In such a solitude my somber way
  Strays like a misanthrope within a gloom
Of his own shadows—till the perfect day
  Bursts into sudden bloom,

And crowns a long, declining stretch of space,
  Where King Corn's armies lie with flags unfurled,
And where the valley's dint in Nature's face
  Dimples a smiling world.

And lo! through mists that may not be dispelled,
  I see an old farm homestead, as in dreams,
Where, like a gem in costly setting held,
    The old log cabin gleams.

*   *   *   *   *   *   *   *   *

O darling Pathway! lead me bravely on
  Adown your valley way, and run before
Among the roses crowding up the lawn
  And thronging at the door,—

And carry up the echo there that shall
  Arouse the drowsy dog, that he may bay
The household out to greet the prodigal
  That wanders home to-day.

ON THE BANKS O' DEER CRICK.

ON the banks o' Deer Crick! There 's the place fer
   me!—
Worter slidin' past ye jes as clair as it kin be:—
See yer shadder in it, and the shadder o' the sky,
And the shadder o' the buzzard as he goes a-lazein' by;
Shadder o' the pizen-vines, and shadder o' the trees—
And I purt'-nigh said the shadder o' the sunshine and
   the breeze!
Well—I never seen the ocean ner I never seen the sea:
On the banks o' Deer Crick 's grand enough fer me!

On the banks o' Deer Crick—mild er two from town—
'Long up where the mill-race comes a-loafin' down,—
Like to git up in there—'mongst the sycamores—
And watch the worter at the dam, a-frothin' as she
   pours:
Crawl out on some old log, with my hook and line,
Where the fish is jes so thick you kin see 'em shine
As they flicker round yer bait, *coaxin'* you to jerk,
Tel yer tired ketchin' of 'em, mighty nigh, as *work!*

On the banks o' Deer Crick!—Allus my delignt
Jes to be around there—take it day er night!—
Watch the snipes and killdees foolin' half the day—
Er these-'ere little worter-bugs skootin' ever'way!—

Snakefeeders glancin' round, er dartin' out o' sight ;
And dew-fall, and bullfrogs, and lightnin'-bugs at
      night—
Stars up through the tree-tops—er in the crick below,—
And smell o' mussrat through the dark clean from the
      old b'y-o!

Er take a tromp, some Sund'y, say, 'way up to
      " Johnson's Hole,"
And find where he's had a fire, and hid his fishin'-pole:
Have yer "dog-leg," with ye and yer pipe and "cut-
      and-dry "—
Pocketful o' corn-bred, and slug er two o' rye,—
Soak yer hide in sunshine and waller in the shade—
Like the Good Book tells us—" where there 're none to
      make afraid!"
Well!—I never seen the ocean ner I never seen the sea—
On the banks o' Deer Crick's grand enough fer me!

A DITTY OF NO TONE—

Piped to the Spirit of John Keats.

I.

WOULD that my lips might pour out in thy praise
    A fitting melody—an air sublime,—
A song sun-washed and draped in dreamy haze—
    The floss and velvet of luxurious rhyme:
A lay wrought of warm languors, and o'er-brimmed
    With balminess, and fragrance of wild flowers
      Such as the droning bee ne'er wearies of—
      Such thoughts as might be hymned
    To thee from this midsummer land of ours
      Through shower and sunshine blent for very love.

II.

Deep silences in woody aisles wherethrough
    Cool paths go loitering, and where the trill
Of best-remembered birds hath something new
    In cadence for the hearing—lingering still
Through all the open day that lies beyond;
    Reaches of pasture-lands, vine-wreathen oaks,
      Majestic still in pathos of decay;—
      The road---the wayside pond
    Wherein the dragonfly an instant soaks
      His filmy wing-tips ere he flits away.

III.

And I would pluck from out the dank, rich mould,
  Thick-shaded from the sun of noon, the long
Lithe stalks of barley, topped with ruddy gold,
  And braid them in the meshes of my song;
And with them I would tangle wheat and rye,
  And wisps of greenest grass the katydid
    Ere crept beneath the blades of, sulkily,
      As harvest-hands went by;
  And weave of all, as wildest fancy bid,
    A crown of mingled song and bloom for thee.

A WATER-COLOR.

L OW hidden in among the forest trees
⎿   An artist's tilted easel, ankle-deep
In tousled ferns and mosses, and in these
  A fluffy water-spaniel, half asleep
    Beside a sketch-book and a fallen hat—
    A little wicker flask tossed into that.

A sense of utter carelessness and grace
  Of pure abandon in the slumb'rous scene,—
As if the June, all hoydenish of face,
  Had romped herself to sleep there on the green,
    And brink and sagging bridge and sliding stream
    Were just romantic parcels of her dream.

THE CYCLONE.

S O lone I stood, the very trees seemed drawn
   In conference with themselves.—Intense—intense
Seemed everything ;—the summer splendor on
   The sight,—magnificence!

A babe's life might not lighter fail and die
   Than failed the sunlight.—Though the hour was noon,
The palm of midnight might not lighter lie
   Upon the brow of June.

With eyes upraised, I saw the underwings
   Of swallows—gone the instant afterward—
While from the elms there came strange twitterings,
   Stilled scarce ere they were heard.

The river seemed to shiver ; and, far down
   Its darkened length, I saw the sycamores
Lean inward closer, under the vast frown
   That weighed above the shores.

Then was a roar, born of some awful burst !—
   And one lay, shrieking, chattering, in my path—
Flung—he or I—out of some space accurst
   As of Jehovah's wrath:

Nor barely had he wreaked his latest prayer,
　Ere back the noon flashed o'er the ruin done,
And, o'er uprooted forests touseled there,
　The birds sang in the sun.

WHERE-AWAY.

O THE Lands of Where-Away!
 Tell us—tell us—where are they?
Through the darkness and the dawn
We have journeyed on and on—
From the cradle to the cross—
From possession unto loss.—
Seeking still, from day to day,
For the lands of Where-Away.

When our baby-feet were first
Planted where the daisies burst,
And the greenest grasses grew
In the fields we wandered through,-
On, with childish discontent,
Ever on and on we went,
Hoping still to pass, some day,
O'er the verge of Where-Away.

Roses laid their velvet lips
On our own, with fragrant sips;
But their kisses held us not,
All their sweetness we forgot;—
Though the brambles in our track
Plucked at us to hold us back—
"Just ahead," we used to say,
"Lie the Lands of Where-Away."

Children at the pasture-bars,
Through the dusk, like glimmering stars,
Waved their hands that we should bide
With them over eventide:
Down the dark their voices failed
Falteringly, as they hailed,
And died into yesterday—
Night ahead and—Where-Away?

Twining arms about us thrown—
Warm caresses, all our own,
Can but stay us for a spell—
Love hath little new to tell
To the soul in need supreme,
Aching ever with the dream
Of the endless bliss it may
Find in Lands of Where-Away!

THE HOME-GOING.

WE must get home—for we have been away
    So long it seems forever and a day!
And O so very homesick we have grown,
The laughter of the world is like a moan
In our tired hearing, and its songs as vain,—
We must get home—we must get home again!

We must get home: It hurts so, staying here,
Where fond hearts must be wept out tear by tear,
And where to wear wet lashes means, at best,
When most our lack, the least our hope of rest—
When most our need of joy, the more our pain—
We must get home—we must get home again!

We must get home: All is so quiet there:
The touch of loving hands on brow and hair—
Dim rooms, wherein the sunshine is made mild—
The lost love of the mother and the child
Restored in restful lullabies of rain.—
We must get home—we must get home again!

We must get home, where, as we nod and
    drowse,
Time humors us and tiptoes through the house,

And loves us best when sleeping baby-wise,
With dreams—not tear-drops—brimming our
　　clenched eyes,—
Pure dreams that know nor taint nor earthly stain—
We must get home—we must get home again !

We must get home; and, unremembering there
All gain of all ambitions otherwhere,
Rest—from the feverish victory, and the crown
Of conquest whose waste glory weighs us down.—
Fame's fairest gifts we toss back with disdain—
We must get home—we must get home again !

HOW JOHN QUIT THE FARM.

NOBODY on the old farm here but Mother, me and
    John,
Except, of course, the extry he'p when harvest-time
    come on—
And then, I want to say to you, we *needed* he'p about,
As you'd admit, ef you'd a-seen the way the crops
    turned out!

A better quarter-section, ner a richer soil warn't found
Than this-here old-home place o' ourn fer fifty miles
    around!—
The house was small—but plenty-big we found it from
    the day
That John—our only livin' son—packed up and went
    away.

You see, we tuck sich pride in John—his mother more 'n
    me—
That's natchurul; but *both* of us was proud as proud
    could be;
Fer the boy, from a little chap, was most oncommon
    bright,
And seemed in work as well as play to take the same
    delight.

He allus went a-whistlin' round the place, as glad at
    heart
As robins up at five o'clock to git an airly start;
And many a time 'fore daylight Mother's waked me up
    to say—
" Jest listen, David!—listen!—Johnny's beat the birds
    to-day!"

High-sperited from boyhood, with a most inquirin' turn,—
He wanted to learn ever'thing on earth they was to
    learn:
He'd ast more plaguey questions in a mortal-minute
    here
Than his grandpap in Paradise could answer in a year!

And *read!* w'y, his own mother learnt him how to read
    and spell;
And "The Childern of the Abbey"—w'y, he knowed
    that book as well
At fifteen as his parents!—and "The Pilgrim's Prog-
    ress," too—
Jest knuckled down, the shaver did, and read 'em
    through and through!

At eighteen, Mother 'lowed the boy must have a better
    chance—
That we ort to educate him, under any circumstance;
And John he j'ined his mother, and they ding-donged
    and kep' on,
Tel I sent him off to school in town, half glad that he
    was gone.

But—I missed him—w'**y,** of course I did!—The Fall and
    Winter through
I never built the kitchen-fire, er split a stick in two,
Er fed the stock, er butchered, er swung up a gambrel-
    pin,
But what I thought o' John, and wished that he was
    home agin.

He 'd come, sometimes—on Sund'ys most—and stay the
    Sund'y out;
And on Thanksgivin'-Day he 'peared to like to be
    about:
But a change was workin' on him—he was stiller than
    before,
And did n't joke, ner laugh, ner sing and whistle any
    more.

And his talk was all so proper; and I noticed, with a
     sigh,
He was tryin' to raise side-whiskers, and had on a
     stripéd tie,
And a standin'-collar, ironed up as stiff and slick as
     bone;
And a breast-pin, and a watch and chain and plug-hat
     of his own.

But when Spring-weather opened out, and John was tu
     come home
And he'p me through the season, I was glad to see
     him come;
But my happiness, that evening, with the settin' sun
     went down,
When he bragged of "a position" that was offered
     him in town.

"But," says I, "you'll not accept it?"   "W'y, of
     course I will," says he.—
"This drudgin' on a farm," he says, "is not the life
     fer me;
I've set my stakes up higher," he continued, light and
     gay,
"And town's the place fer *me*, and I'm a-goin' right
     away!"

And go he did!—his mother clingin' to him at the
    gate,
A-pleadin' and a-cryin'; but it had n't any weight.
I was tranquiller, and told her 't warn't no use to
    worry so,
And onclasped her arms from round his neck round
    mine—and let him go!

I felt a little bitter feelin' foolin' round about
The aidges of my conscience; but I did n't let it out;—
I simply retch out, trimbly-like, and tuck the boy's
    hand,
And though I did n't say a word, I knowed he 'd
    understand.

And—well!—sence then the old home here was mighty
    lonesome, shore!
With me a-workin' in the field, and Mother at the
    door,
Her face ferever to'rds the town, and fadin' more and
    more—
Her only son nine miles away, a-clerkin' in a store!

The weeks and months dragged by us; and sometimes
    the boy would write
A letter to his mother, sayin' that his work was light,
And not to feel oneasy about his health a bit—
Though his business was confinin', he was gittin' used
    to it.

And sometimes he would write and ast how *I* was
    gittin' on,
And ef I had to pay out much fer he'p sence he was
    gone;
And how the hogs was doin', and the balance of the
    stock,
And talk on fer a page er two jest like he used to
    talk.

And he wrote, along 'fore harvest, that he guessed he
    would git home,
Fer business would, of course be dull in town.—But
    didn't come:—
We got a postal later, sayin' when they had no trade
They filled the time "invoicin' goods," and that was
    why he staid.

And then he quit a-writin' altogether: Not a word—
Exceptin' what the neighbers brung who'd been to
    town and heard
What store John was clerkin' in, and went round to
    inquire
If they could buy their goods there less and sell their
    produce higher.

And so the Summer faded out, and Autumn wore
    away,
And a keener Winter never fetched around Thanks-
    givin'-Day!
The night before that day of thanks I'll never quite
    fergit,
The wind a-howlin' round the house—it makes me
    creepy yit!

And there set me and Mother—me a-twistin' at the
    prongs
Of a green scrub-ellum forestick with a vicious pair of
    tongs,
And Mother sayin', "*David! David!*" in a' undertone,
As though she thought that I was thinkin' bad-words
    unbeknown.

"I've dressed the turkey, David, fer to-morrow,"
      Mother said,
A-tryin' to wedge some pleasant subject in my stubborn
      head,—
"And the mince-meat I'm a mixin' is perfection mighty
      nigh ;
And the pound-cake is delicious-rich—" "Who'll eat
      'em?" I-says-I.

"The cramberries is drippin -sweet," says Mother,
      runnin' on,
P'tendin' not to hear me;—"and somehow I thought
      of John
All the time they was a-jellin'—fer you know they
      allus was
His favorite—he likes 'em so!" Says I, "Well, s'pose
      he does?"

"Oh, nothin' much!" says Mother, with a quiet sort
      o' smile—
"This gentleman behind my cheer may tell you after
      while!"
And as I turned and looked around, some one riz up
      and leant
And put his arms round Mother's neck, and laughed in
      low content.

"It 's *me*," he says—"your fool-boy John, come back
    to shake your hand ;
Set down with you, and talk with you, and make you
    understand
How dearer yit than all the world is this old home
    that we
Will spend Thanksgivin' in fer life—jest Mother, you
    and me!"

*   *   *   *   *   *   *

Nobody on the old farm here but Mother, me and John,
Except of course the extry he'p, when harvest-time
    comes on ;
And then, I want to say to you, we *need* sich he'p
    about,
As you 'd admit, ef you could see the way the crops
    turns out !

NORTH AND SOUTH.

OF the North I wove a dream,
  All bespangled with the gleam
Of the glancing wings of swallows
Dipping ripples in a stream,
That, like a tide of wine,
Wound through lands of shade and shine
Where purple grapes hung bursting on the vine.

And where orchard-boughs were bent
Till their tawny fruitage blent
  With the golden wake that marked the
Way the happy reapers went;
Where the dawn died into noon
As the May-mists into June,
And the dusk fell like a sweet face in a swoon.

Of the South I dreamed: And there
Came a vision clear and fair
  As the marvelous enchantments
Of the mirage of the air;
And I saw the bayou-trees,
With their lavish draperies,
Hang heavy o'er the moon-washed cypress-knees.

Peering from lush fens of rice,
I beheld the Negro's eyes,
  Lit with that old superstition
Death itself can not disguise;
And I saw the palm tree nod
Like an oriental god,
And the cotton froth and bubble from the pod

And I dreamed that North and South,
With a sigh of dew and drouth,
  Blew each unto the other
The salute of lip and mouth;
And I wakened, awed and thrilled—
Every doubting murmur stilled
In the silence of the dream I found fulfilled.

THE IRON HORSE.

NO song is mine of Arab steed—
　　My courser is of nobler blood,
And cleaner limb and fleeter speed,
　　And greater strength and hardihood
Than ever cantered wild and free
Across the plains of Araby.

Go search the level desert-land
From Sana on to Samarcand—
Wherever Persian prince has been
Or Dervish, Sheik or Bedouin,
And I defy you there to point
　　Me out a steed the half so fine—
From tip of ear to pastern-joint—
　　As this old iron horse of mine.

You do not know what beauty is—
　　You do not know what gentleness
　　His answer is to my caress!—
Why, look upon this gait of his,—
A touch upon his iron rein—
　　He moves with such a stately grace
The sunlight on his burnished mane
　　Is barely shaken in its place;
　　And at touch he changes pace,
And, gliding backward, stops again.

And talk of mettle—Ah! my friend,
  Such passion smoulders in his breast
That when awakened it will send
  A thrill of rapture wilder than
  Ere palpitated heart of man
  When flaming at its mightiest.
And there's a fierceness in his ire—
  A maddened majesty that leaps
Along his veins in blood of fire,
  Until the path his vision sweeps
Spins out behind him like a thread
  Unraveled from the reel of time,
  As, wheeling on his course sublime,
The earth revolves beneath his tread.

Then stretch away, my gallant steed!
  Thy mission is a noble one:
  You bear the father to the son,
And sweet relief to bitter need;
You bear the stranger to his friends;
  You bear the pilgrim to the shrine,
And back again the prayer he sends
  That God will prosper me and mine,—
The star that on thy forehead gleams
Has blossomed in our brightest dreams.
Then speed thee on thy glorious race!
The mother waits thy ringing pace;

The father leans an anxious ear
The thunder of thy hoofs to hear;
The lover listens, far away,
To catch thy keen exultant neigh;
And, where thy breathings roll and rise,
The husband strains his eager eyes,
And laugh of wife and baby-glee
Ring out to greet and welcome thee.
Then stretch away! and when at last
  The master's hand shall gently check
Thy mighty speed, and hold thee fast,
  The world will pat thee on the neck.

HIS MOTHER'S WAY

TOMPS 'ud allus haf to say
   Somepin' 'bout "his mother's way."—
He lived hard-like—never jined
Any church of any kind.—
"It was Mother's way," says he,
"To be good enough fer *me*
  And her too,—and certinly
     Lord has heerd *her* pray!"
Propped up on his dyin' bed,—
"Shore as Heaven 's overhead,
  I'm a-goin' there," he said—
    "It was Mother's way."

JAP MILLER.

JAP MILLER down at Martinsville's the blamedest
feller yit!
When *he* starts in a-talkin' other folks is apt to quit!—
'Pears like that mouth o' his'n wuz n't made fer nuthin'
else
But jes' to argify 'em down and gether in their pelts:
He'll talk you down on tariff; er he'll talk you down
on tax,
And prove the pore man pays 'em all—and them's
about the fac's!—
Religen, law, er politics, prize-fightin', er base-ball—
Jes' tetch Jap up a little and he'll post you 'bout 'em
all.

And the comicalist feller ever tilted back a cheer
And tuck a chaw tobacker kind o' like he did n't keer.—
There's where the feller's stren'th lays,—he's so com-
mon-like and plain,—
They haint no dude about old Jap, you bet you—nary
grain!
They 'lected him to Council and it never turned his
head,
And did n't make no differunce what anybody said,—
He did n't dress no finer, ner rag out in fancy clothes;
But his voice in Council-meetin's is a turrer to his foes.

He's fer the pore man ever' time!   And in the last
    campaign
He stumped old Morgan County, through the sunshine
    and the rain,
And helt the banner up'ards from a-trailin' in the dust,
And cut loose on monopolies and cuss'd and cuss'd and
    cuss'd!
He'd tell some funny story ever' now and then, you
    know,
Tel, blame it! it wuz better 'n a jack-o'-lantern show!
And I'd go furder, yit, to-day, to hear old Jap norate
Than any high-toned orator 'at ever stumped the State!

W'y, that-air blame Jap Miller, with his keen sircastic
    fun,
Has got more friends than ary candidate 'at ever run!
Don't matter what *his* views is, when he states the
    same to you,
They allus coincide with your 'n, the same as two and
    two:
You *can't* take issue with him—er, at least, they haint
    no sense
In startin' in to down him, so you better not commence.—
The best way 's jes' to listen, like your humble servant
    does,
And jes' concede Jap Miller is the best man ever wuz!

A SOUTHERN SINGER.

Written in Madison Cawein's "Lyrics and Idyls."

HEREIN are blown from out the South
    Songs blithe as those of Pan's pursed
        mouth—
As sweet in voice as, in perfume,
The night-breath of magnolia-bloom.

Such sumptuous languor lures the sense—
Such luxury of indolence—
The eyes blur as a nymph's might blur,
With water-lilies watching her.

You waken, thrilling at the trill
Of some wild bird that seems to spill
The silence full of winey drips
Of song that Fancy sips and sips.

Betimes, in brambled lanes wherethrough
The chipmunk stripes himself from view,
You pause to lop a creamy spray
Of elder-blossoms by the way.

Or where the morning dew is yet
Gray on the topmost rail, you set
A sudden palm and, vaulting, meet
Your vaulting shadow in the wheat.

On lordly swards, of suave incline,
Entessellate with shade and shine,
You shall misdoubt your lowly birth,
Clad on as one of princely worth:

The falcon on your wrist shall ride—
Your milk-white Arab side by side
With one of raven-black.—You fain
Would kiss the hand that holds the rein.

Nay, nay, Romancer! Poet! Seer!
Sing us back home—from there to here:
Grant your high grace and wit, but we
Most honor your simplicity.—

Herein are blown from out the South
Songs blithe as those of Pan's pursed mouth—
As sweet in voice as, in perfume,
The night-breath of magnolia-bloom.

A DREAM OF AUTUMN.

MELLOW hazes, lowly trailing
    Over wood and meadow, veiling
Somber skies, with wildfowl sailing
    Sailor-like to foreign lands;
And the north-wind overleaping
Summer's brink, and floodlike sweeping
Wrecks of roses where the weeping
    Willows wring their helpless hands.

Flared, like Titan torches flinging
Flakes of flame and embers, springing
From the vale the trees stand swinging
    In the moaning atmosphere;
While in dead'ning-lands the lowing
Of the cattle, sadder growing,
Fills the sense to overflowing
    With the sorrow of the year.

Sorrowfully, yet the sweeter
Sings the brook in rippled meter
Under boughs that lithely teeter
    Lorn birds, answering from the shores
Through the viny, shady-shiny
Interspaces, shot with tiny
Flying motes that fleck the winy
    Wave-engraven sycamores.

Fields of ragged stubble, wrangled
With rank weeds, and shocks of tangled
Corn, with crests like rent plumes dangled
  Over Harvest's battle-plain;
And the sudden whir and whistle
Of the quail that, like a missile,
Whizzes over thorn and thistle,
  And, a missile, drops again.

Muffled voices, hid in thickets
Where the redbird stops to stick its
Ruddy beak betwixt the pickets
  Of the truant's rustic trap;
And the sound of laughter ringing
Where, within the wild-vine swinging,
Climb Bacchante's schoolmates, flinging
  Purple clusters in her lap.

Rich as wine, the sunset flashes
Round the tilted world, and dashes
Up the sloping west and splashes
  Red foam over sky and sea—
Till my dream of Autumn, paling
In the splendor all-prevailing,
Like a sallow leaf goes sailing
  Down the silence solemnly.

TOM VAN ARDEN.

TOM VAN ARDEN, my old friend,
  Our warm fellowship is one
Far too old to comprehend
  Where its bond was first begun:
    Mirage-like before my gaze
    Gleams a land of other days,
    Where two truant boys, astray,
    Dream their lazy lives away.

There's a vision, in the guise
  Of Midsummer, where the Past
Like a weary beggar lies
  In the shadow Time has cast;
    And as blends the bloom of trees
    With the drowsy hum of bees,
    Fragrant thoughts and murmurs blend,
    Tom Van Arden, my old friend.

Tom Van Arden, my old friend,
  All the pleasures we have known
Thrill me now as I extend
  This old hand and grasp your own—
    Feeling, in the rude caress,
    All affection's tenderness;
    Feeling, though the touch be rough,
    Our old souls are soft enough.

So we 'll make a mellow hour:
  Fill your pipe, and taste the wine—
Warp your face, if it be sour,
  I can spare a smile from mine;
    If it sharpen up your wit,
    Let me feel the edge of it—
    I have eager ears to lend,
    Tom Van Arden, my old friend.

Tom Van Arden, my old friend,
  Are we "lucky dogs," indeed?
Are we all that we pretend
  In the jolly life we lead?—
    Bachelors, we must confess,
    Boast of "single blessedness"
    To the world, but not alone—
    Man's best sorrow is his own!

And the saddest truth is this,—
  Life to us has never proved
What we tasted in the kiss
  Of the women we have loved:
    Vainly we congratulate
    Our escape from such a fate
    As their lying lips could send,
    Tom Van Arden, my old friend!

Tom Van Arden, my old friend,
  Hearts, like fruit upon the stem,
Ripen sweetest, I contend,
  As the frost falls over them:
    Your regard for me to-day
    Makes November taste of May,
    And through every vein of rhyme
    Pours the blood of summertime.

When our souls are cramped with youth
  Happiness seems far away
In the future, while, in truth,
  We look back on it to-day
    Through our tears, nor dare to boast,—
    "Better to have loved and lost!"
    Broken hearts are hard to mend,
    Tom Van Arden, my old friend.

Tom Van Arden, my old friend,
  I grow prosy, and you tire;
Fill the glasses while I bend
  To prod up the failing fire. . .
    You are restless:—I presume
    There's a dampness in the room.—
    Much of warmth our nature begs,
    With rheumatics in our legs!...

Humph! the legs we used to fling
  Limber-jointed in the dance,
When we heard the fiddle ring
  Up the curtain of Romance,
    And in crowded public halls
    Played with hearts like jugglers'-balls.—
    Feats of mountebanks, depend!—
    Tom Van Arden, my old friend.

Tom Van Arden, my old friend,
  Pardon, then, this theme of mine:
While the fire-light leaps to lend
  Higher color to the wine,—
    I propose a health to those
    Who have *homes*, and home's repose,
    Wife- and child-love without end!
    ... Tom Van Arden, my old friend.

JUST TO BE GOOD.

JUST to be good—
       This is enough—enough!
O we who find sin's billows wild and rough,
Do we not feel how more than any gold
Would be the blameless life we led of old
While yet our lips knew but a mother's kiss?
       Ah! though we miss
       All else but this,
              To be good is enough!

It is enough—
       Enough—just to be good!
To lift our hearts where they are understood;
To let the thirst for worldly power and place
Go unappeased; to smile back in God's face
With the glad lips our mothers used to kiss.
       Ah! though we miss
       All else but this,
              To be good is enough!

HOME AT NIGHT.

WHEN chirping crickets fainter cry,
　　And pale stars blossom in the sky,
And twilight's gloom has dimmed the bloom
And blurred the butterfly:

When locust-blossoms fleck the walk,
And up the tiger-lily stalk
The glow-worm crawls and clings and falls
And glimmers down the garden-walls:

When buzzing things, with double wings
Of crisp and raspish flutterings,
Go whizzing by so very nigh
One thinks of fangs and stings:—

O then, within, is stilled the din
Of crib she rocks the baby in,
And heart and gate and latch's weight
Are lifted—and the lips of Kate.

THE HOOSIER FOLK-CHILD.

THE Hoosier Folk-Child—all unsung—
    Unlettered all of mind and tongue;
Unmastered, unmolested—made
Most wholly frank and unafraid:
Untaught of any school—unvexed
Of law or creed—all unperplexed—
Unsermoned, aye, and undefiled,
An all imperfect-perfect child—
A type which (Heaven forgive us!) you
And I do tardy honor to,
And so, profane the sanctities
Of our most sacred memories.
Who, growing thus from boy to man,
That dares not be American?
Go, Pride, with prudent underbuzz—
Go *whistle!* as the Folk-Child does.

The Hoosier Folk-Child's world is not
Much wider than the stable-lot
Between the house and highway fence
That bounds the home his father rents.
His playmates mostly are the ducks
And chickens, and the boy that "shucks

Corn by the shock," and talks of town,
And whether eggs are "up" or "down,"
And prophesies in boastful tone
Of "owning horses of his own,"
And "being his own man," and "when
He gets to be, what he'll do then."—
Takes out his jack-knife dreamily
And makes the Folk-Child two or three
Crude corn-stalk figures,—a wee span
Of horses and a little man.

The Hoosier Folk-Child's eyes are wise
And wide and round as Brownies' eyes:
The smile they wear is ever blent
With all-expectant wonderment,—
On homeliest things they bend a look
As rapt as o'er a picture-book,
And seem to ask, whate'er befall,
The happy reason of it all:—
Why grass is all so glad a green,
And leaves—and what their lispings mean ;—
Why buds grow on the boughs, and why
They burst in blossom by and by—
As though the orchard in the breeze
Had shook and popped its *popcorn-trees*,
To lure and whet, as well they might,
Some seven-league giant's appetite!

The Hoosier Folk-Child's chubby face
Has scant refinement, caste or grace,—
From crown to chin, and cheek to cheek,
It bears the grimy water-streak
Of rinsings such as some long rain
Might drool across the window-pane
Wherethrough he peers, with troubled frown,
As some lorn team drives by for town.
His brow is elfed with wispish hair,
With tangles in it here and there,
As though the warlocks snarled it so
At midmirk when the moon sagged low,
And boughs did toss and skreek and shake,
And children moaned themselves awake,
With fingers clutched, and starting sight
Blind as the blackness of the night!

The Hoosier Folk-Child!—Rich is he
In all the wealth of poverty!
He owns nor title nor estate,
Nor speech but half articulate,—
He owns nor princely robe nor crown ;—
Yet, draped in patched and faded brown,
He owns the bird-songs of the hills—
The laughter of the April rills;
And his are all the diamonds set
In Morning's dewy coronet,—

And his the Dusk's first minted stars
That twinkle through the pasture-bars,
And litter all the skies at night
With glittering scraps of silver light;—
The rainbow's bar, from rim to rim,
In beaten gold, belongs to him.

JACK THE GIANT KILLER.

Bad Boy's Version.

TELL you a story—an' it's a fac':—
   Wunst wuz a little boy, name wuz Jack,
An' he had sword an' buckle an' strap
Maked of gold, an' a "'visibul cap;"
An' he killed Gi'nts 'at et whole cows—
Th' horns an' all—an' pigs an' sows!
But Jack, his golding sword wuz, oh!
So awful sharp 'at he could go
An' cut th' ole Gi'nts clean in two
Fore 'ey knowed what he wuz goin' to do!
An' *one* ole Gi'nt, he had four
Heads, and name wuz "Bumblebore"—
An' he wuz feered o' Jack—'cause he,
Jack, he killed six—five—ten—three,
An' all o' th' uther ole Gi'nts but him:
An' thay wuz a place Jack haf to swim
'Fore he could git t' ole "Bumblebore"—
Nen thay was "griffuns" at the door:
But Jack, he thist plunged in an' swum
Clean acrost; an' when he come

1o th' uther side, he thist put on
His "'visibul cap," an' nen, dog-gone!
You could n't see him at all!—An' so
He slewed the "griffuns"—*boff*, you know!
Nen wuz a horn hunged over his head,
High on th' wall, an' words 'at read,—
"Whoever kin this trumput blow
Shall cause the Gi'nt's overth'ow!"
An' Jack, he thist reached up an' blowed
The stuffin' out of it! an' th'owed
Th' castul-gates wide open, an'
Nen tuck his gold sword in his han',
An' thist marched in t' ole "Bumblebore,"
An', 'fore he knowed, he put 'bout four
Heads on him—an' chopped 'em off, too!—·
Wisht 'at *I'd* been Jack!—don't you?

WHILE THE MUSICIAN PLAYED.

O IT was but a dream I had
  While the musician played!—
And here the sky, and here the glad
  Old ocean kissed the glade—
And here the laughing ripples ran,
  And here the roses grew
That threw a kiss to every man
  That voyaged with the crew.

Our silken sails in lazy folds
  Drooped in the breathless breeze:
As o'er a field of marigolds
  Our eyes swam o'er the seas;
While here the eddies lisped and purled
  Around the island's rim,
And up from out the underworld
  We saw the mermen swim.

And it was dawn and middle-day
  And midnight—for the moon
On silver rounds across the bay
  Had climbed the skies of June—
And there the glowing, glorious king
  Of day ruled o'er his realm,
With stars of midnight glittering
  About his diadem.

The seagull reeled on languid wing
  In circles round the mast,
We heard the songs the sirens sing
  As we went sailing past;
And up and down the golden sands
  A thousand fairy throngs
Flung at us from their flashing hands
  The echoes of their songs.

O it was but a dream I had
  While the musician played—
For here the sky, and here the glad
  Old ocean kissed the glade;
And here the laughing ripples ran,
  And here the roses grew
That threw a kiss to every man
  That voyaged with the crew.

AUGUST.

A DAY of torpor in the sullen heat
 Of Summer's passion: In the sluggish stream
The panting cattle lave their lazy feet,
 With drowsy eyes, and dream.

Long since the winds have died, and in the sky
 There lives no cloud to hint of Nature's grief ;
The sun glares ever like an evil eye,
 And withers flower and leaf.

Upon the gleaming harvest-field remote
 The thresher lies deserted, like some old
Dismantled galleon that hangs afloat
 Upon a sea of gold.

The yearning cry of some bewildered bird
 Above an empty nest, and truant boys
Along the river's shady margin heard—
 A harmony of noise—

A melody of wrangling voices blent
 With liquid laughter, and with rippling calls
Of piping lips and trilling echoes sent
 To mimic waterfalls.

And through the hazy veil the atmosphere
  Has draped about the gleaming face of Day,
The sifted glances of the sun appear
  In splinterings of spray.

The dusty highway, like a cloud of dawn,
  Trails o'er the hillside, and the passer-by,
A tired ghost in misty shroud, toils on
  His journey to the sky.

And down across the valley's drooping sweep,
  Withdrawn to farthest limit of the glade,
The forest stands in silence, drinking deep
  Its purple wine of shade.

The gossamer floats up on phantom wing ;
  The sailor-vision voyages the skies
And carries into chaos everything
  That freights the weary eyes :

Till, throbbing on and on, the pulse of heat
  Increases—reaches—passes fever's height,
And Day sinks into slumber, cool and sweet,
  Within the arms of Night.

TO HEAR HER SING.

TO hear her sing—to hear her sing-
It is to hear the birds of Spring
In dewy groves on blooming sprays
Pour out their blithest roundelays.

It is to hear the robin trill
At morning, or the whip-poor-will
At dusk, when stars are blossoming—
To hear her sing—to hear her sing!

To hear her sing—it is to hear
The laugh of childhood ringing clear
In woody path or grassy lane
Our feet may never fare again.

Faint, far away as Memory dwells,
It is to hear the village bells
At twilight, as the truant hears
Them, hastening home, with smiles and tears.

Such joy it is to hear her sing,
We fall in love with everything—
The simple things of every day
Grow lovelier than words can say.

The idle brooks that purl across
The gleaming pebbles and the moss,
We love no less than classic streams—
The Rhines and Arnos of our dreams.

To hear her sing—with folded eyes,
It is, beneath Venetian skies,
To hear the gondoliers' refrain,
Or troubadours of sunny Spain.—

To hear the bulbul's voice that shook
The throat that trilled for Lalla Rookh:
What wonder we in homage bring
Our hearts to her—to hear her sing!

BEING HIS MOTHER.

BEING his mother,—when he goes away
    I would not hold him overlong, and so
  Sometimes my yielding sight of him grows O
So quick of tears, I joy he did not stay
To catch the faintest rumor of them! Nay,
    Leave always his eyes clear and glad, although
    Mine own, dear Lord, do fill to overflow;
Let his remembered features, as I pray,
Smile ever on me! Ah! what stress of love
    Thou givest me to guard with Thee thiswise:
    Its fullest speech ever to be denied
Mine own—being his mother! All thereof
    Thou knowest only, looking from the skies
    As when not Christ alone was crucified.

JUNE AT WOODRUFF.

OUT at Woodruff Place—afar
　From the city's glare and jar,
With the leafy trees, instead
Of the awnings, overhead;
With the shadows cool and sweet,
For the fever of the street;
With the silence, like a prayer,
Breathing round us everywhere.

Gracious anchorage, at last,
From the billows of the vast
Tide of life that comes and goes,
Whence and where nobody knows—
Moving, like a skeptic's thought,
Out of nowhere into naught.
Touch and tame us with thy grace,
Placid calm of Woodruff Place!

Weave a wreath of beechen leaves
For the brow that throbs and grieves
O'er the ledger, bloody-lined,
'Neath the sun-struck window-blind!
Send the breath of woodland bloom
Through the sick man's prison room,
Till his old farm-home shall swim
Sweet in mind to hearten him!

Out at Woodruff Place the Muse
Dips her sandal in the dews,
Sacredly as night and dawn
Baptize lilied grove and lawn:
Woody path, or paven way—
She doth haunt them night and day,—
Sun or moonlight through the trees,
To her eyes, are melodies.

Swinging lanterns, twinkling clear
Through night-scenes, are songs to her—
Tinted lilts and choiring hues,
Blent with children's glad halloos;
Then belated lays that fade
Into midnight's serenade—
Vine-like words and zithern-strings
Twined through all her slumberings.

Blessèd be each hearthstone set
Neighboring the violet!
Blessèd every rooftree prayed
Over by the beech's shade!
Blessèd doorway, opening where
We may look on Nature—there
Hand to hand and face to face—
Storied realm, or Woodruff Place.

FARMER WHIPPLE.—BACHELOR.

IT 'S a mystery to see me—a man o' fifty-four,
  Who 's lived a cross old bachelor fer thirty year'
    and more—
A-lookin' glad and smilin'! And they 's none o' you
    can say
That you can guess the reason why I feel so good
    to-day!

I must tell you all about it! But I 'll have to deviate
A little in beginnin', so 's to set the matter straight
As to how it comes to happen that I never took a
    wife—
Kind o' "crawfish" from the Present to the Springtime
    of my life!

I was brought up in the country: Of a family of
    five—
Three brothers and a sister—I 'm the only one alive,—
Fer they all died little babies; and 'twas one o'
    Mother's ways,
You know, to want a daughter; so she took a girl to
    raise.

The sweetest little thing she was, with rosy cheeks,
       and fat—
We was little chunks o' shavers then about as high as
       that!
But someway we sort o' *suited*-like! and Mother she'd
       declare
She never laid her eyes on a more lovin' pair

Than *we* was! So we growed up side by side fer
       thirteen year',
And every hour of it she growed to me more dear!—
W'y, even Father's dyin', as he did, I do believe
War n't more affectin' to me than it was to see her
       grieve!

I was then a lad o' twenty; and I felt a flash o' pride
In thinkin' all depended on *me* now to pervide
Fer Mother and fer Mary; and I went about the place
With sleeves rolled up—and workin', with a mighty
       smilin' face.—

Fer *sompin' else* was workin'! but not a word I said
Of a certain sort o' notion that was runnin' through
       my head,—
"Someday I'd mayby marry, and *a brother's* love was one
Thing—*a lover's* was another!" was the way the notion
       run!

I remember onc't in harvest, when the "cradle-in'" was
    done—
When the harvest of my summers mounted up to
    twenty-one—
I was ridin' home with Mary at the closin' o' the day—
A-chawin' straws and thinkin', in a lover's lazy way!

And Mary's cheeks was burnin' like the sunset down
    the lane:
I noticed she was thinkin', too, and ast her to explain.
Well—when she turned and *kissed* me, *with her arms
    around me—law!*
I'd a bigger load o' heaven than I had a load o' straw!

I don't p'tend to learnin', but I'll tell you what's a
    fac',
They's a mighty truthful sayin' somers in a
    almanack —
Er *somers*—'bout "puore happiness"—perhaps some
    folks 'll laugh
At the idy—"only lastin' jest two seconds and a
    half."—

But its jest as true as preachin'!—fer that was *a sister's*
    kiss,
And a sister's lovin' confidence a-tellin' to me this:—

" *She* was happy, *bein' promised to the son o' farmer
    Brown.*"—
And my feelin's struck a pardnership with sunset anJ
    went down!

I do n't know *how* I acted—I don't know *what* I said,
Fer my heart seemed jest a-turnin' to an ice-cold lump
    o' lead;
And the hosses kindo' glimmered before me in the road,
And the lines fell from my fingers—and that was all I
    knowed—

Fer—well, I do n't know *how* long—They's a dim remem-
    berence
Of a sound o' snortin' hosses, and a stake-and-ridered
    fence
A-whizzin' past, and wheat-sheaves a-dancin' in the air,
And Mary screamin' "Murder!" and a-runnin' up to
    where

I was layin' by the roadside, and the wagon upside
    down
A-leanin' on the gate-post, with the wheels a whirlin'
    round!
And I tried to raise and meet her, but I could n't, with
    a vague
Sorto' notion comin' to me that I had a broken leg.

Well, the women nussed me through it; but many a
  time I'd sigh
As I'd keep a-gittin' better instid o' goin' to die,
And wonder what was left *me* worth livin' fer below,
When the girl I loved was married to another, do n't
  you know!

And my thoughts was as rebellious as the folks was
  good and kind
When Brown and Mary married—Railly must a-been my
  mind
Was kindo' out o' kilter!—fer I hated Brown, you see,
Worse'n *pizen*—and the feller whittled crutches out fer
  me—

And done a thousand little ac's o' kindness and
  respec'—
And me a-wishin' all the time that I could break his
  neck!
My relief was like a mourner's when the funeral is
  done
When they moved to Illinois in the Fall o' Forty-one.

Then I went to work in airnest—I had nothin' much in
  view
But to drownd out rickollections—and it kep' me busy,
  too!

But I slowly thrived and prospered, tel Mother used to
    say
She expected yit to see me a wealthy man some day.

Then I 'd think how little *money* was, compared to
    happiness—
And who 'd be left to use it when I died I could n 't
    guess !
But I 've still kep ' speculatin' and a-gainin' year by
    year,
Tel I 'm payin' half the taxes in the county, mighty
    near !

Well !—A year ago er better, a letter comes to hand
Astin' how I 'd like to dicker fer some Illinois land—
" The feller that had owned it," it went ahead to state,
" Had jest deceased, insolvent, leavin' chance to
    speculate,"—

And then it closed by sayin' that I 'd " better come and
    see."—
I 'd never been West, anyhow—a most too wild fer *me*,
I 'd allus had a notion ; but a lawyer here in town
Said I 'd find myself mistakend when I come to look
    around.

So I bids good-bye to Mother, and I jumps aboard the
    train,
A-thinkin' what I'd bring her when I come back home
    again—
And ef she'd had an idy what the present was to be,
I think it's more 'n likely she'd a-went along with me!

Cars is awful tejus ridin', fer all they go so fast!
But finally they called out my stoppin'-place at last:
And that night, at the tavern, I dreamp' I was a train
O' cars, and *skeered* at sumpin', runnin' down a country
    lane!

Well, in the mornin' airly—after huntin' up the man—
The lawyer who was wantin' to swap the piece o' land—
We started fer the country; and I ast the history
Of the farm—its former owner—and so-forth, etcetery!

And—well—it was *interestin'*—I su'prised him, I suppose,
By the loud and frequent manner in which I blowed my
    nose!—
But his su'prise was greater, and it made him wonder
    more,
When I kissed and hugged the widder when she met
    us at the door!—

It was Mary : They's a feelin' a-hidin' down in here—
Of course I can't explain it, ner ever make it clear.—
It was with us in that meetin', I don't want you to
     fergit !
And it makes me kind o' nervous when I think about
     it yit !

I *bought* that farm, and *deeded* it, afore I left the town,
With "title clear to mansions in the skies," to Mary
     Brown !
And fu'thermore, I took her and *the childern*—fer you
     see,
They'd never seed their Grandma—and I fetched 'em
     home with me.

So *now* you've got an idy why a man o' fifty-four,
Who's lived a cross old bachelor fer thirty year' and
     more,
Is a-lookin' glad and smilin'!—And I've jest come into
     town
To git a pair o' license fer to *marry* Mary Brown.

DAWN, NOON AND DEWFALL.

I.

DAWN, noon and dewfall! Bluebird and robin
    Up and at it airly, and the orchard-blossoms
    bobbin'!
Peekin' from the winder, half-awake, and wishin'
I could go to sleep agin as well as go a-fishin'!

II.

On the apern o' the dam, legs a-danglin' over,
Drowsy-like with sound o' worter and the smell o'
    clover:
Fish all out a visitin'—'cept some dratted minnor!
Yes, and mill shet down at last and hands is gone to
    dinner.

III.

Trompin' home acrost the fields: Lightnin'-bugs a-
    blinkin'
In the wheat like sparks o' things feller keeps a-
    thinkin':—
Mother waitin' supper, and the childern there to
    cherr me!
And fiddle on the kitchen-wall a-jist a-eechin' fer me!

NESSMUK.

I HAIL thee, Nessmuk, for the lofty tone
   Yet simple grace that marks thy poetry!
   True forester thou art, and still to be,
Even in happier fields than thou hast known.
Thus, in glad visions, glimpses am I shown
     Of groves delectable—"preserves" for thee—
     Ranged but by friends of thine—I name thee
        three:—
First, Chaucer, with his bald old pate new-grown
   With changeless laurel; next, in Lincoln-green,
     Gold-belted, bowed and bugled, Robin Hood;
   And next, Ike Walton, patient and serene:
These three, O Nessmuk, gathered hunter-wise,
Are camped on hither slopes of Paradise
     To hail thee first and greet thee, as they should.

AS MY UNCLE USED TO SAY.

I 'VE thought a power on men and things,
   As my uncle ust to say,—
And ef folks don't work as they pray, i jings!
   W'y, they ain't no use to pray!
Ef you want somepin', and jes dead-set
A-pleadin' fer it with both eyes wet,
And *tears* won't bring it, w'y, you try *sweat*,
   As my uncle ust to say.

They 's some don't know their A, B, Cs,
   As my uncle ust to say,
And yit don't waste no candle-grease,
   Ner whistle their lives away!
But ef they can't write no book, ner rhyme
No ringin' song fer to last all time,
They can blaze the way fer the march sublime,
   As my uncle ust to say.

Whoever 's Foreman of all things here,
   As my uncle ust to say,
He knows each job 'at we 're best fit fer,
   And our round-up, night and day:
And a-sizin' *His* work, east and west,
And north and south, and worst and best
I ain't got nothin' to suggest,
   As my uncle ust to say.

THE SINGER.

WHILE with Ambition's hectic flame
　　He wastes the midnight oil,
And dreams, high-throned on heights of fame,
　To rest him from his toil,—

Death's Angel, like a vast eclipse,
　Above him spreads her wings,
And fans the embers of his lips
　To ashes as he sings.

A FULL HARVEST.

SEEMS like a feller 'd ort 'o jes' to-day
  Git down and roll and waller, don't you know,
 In that-air stubble, and flop up and crow,
Seein' sich craps! I 'll undertake to say
There 're no wheat 's ever turned out thataway
  Afore this season!—Folks is keerless tho',
  And too fergitful—'caze we 'd ort 'o show
More thankfulness!—Jes' looky hyonder, hey?—
  And watch that little reaper wadin' thue
That last old yaller hunk o' harvest-ground—
  Jes' natchur'ly a-slicin' it in-two
Like honey-comb, and gaumin' it around
  The field—like it had nothin' else to do
  On'y jes' waste it all on me and you!

BLIND.

YOU think it is a sorry thing
    That I am blind. Your pitying
Is welcome to me; yet indeed,
I think I have but little need
Of it. Though you may marvel much
That *we*, who see by sense of touch
And taste and hearing, see things *you*
May never look upon; and true
Is it that even in the scent
Of blossoms *we* find something meant
No eyes have in their faces read,
Or wept to see interpreted.

And you might think it strange if now
I told you you were smiling. How
Do I know that? I hold your hand—
Its language I can understand—
Give both to me, and i will show
You many other things I know.
Listen: We never met before
Till now?—Well, you are something lower
Than five-feet-eight in height; and you
Are slender; and your eyes are blue—

Your mother's eyes—your mother's hair—
Your mother's likeness everywhere
Save in your walk—and that is quite
Your father's; nervous.—Am I right?
I thought so. And you used to sing,
But have neglected everything
Of vocalism—though you may
Still thrum on the guitar, and play
A little on the violin,—
I know that by the callous in
The finger-tips of your left hand—
And, by-the-bye, though nature planned
You as most men, you are, I see,
"*Left*-handed," too,—the mystery
Is clear, though,—your right arm has been
Broken, to "break" the left one in.
And so, you see, though blind of sight,
I still have ways of seeing quite
Too well for you to sympathize
Excessively, with your good eyes.—
Though *once*, perhaps, to be sincere,
Within the whole asylum here,
From cupola to basement hall,
I was the blindest of them all!

Let us move further down the walk—
The man here waiting hears my talk,

And is disturbed; besides, he may
Not be quite friendly anyway.
In fact—(this will be far enough;
Sit down)—the man just spoken of
Was once a friend of mine. He came
For treatment here from Burlingame—
A rich though brilliant student there,
Who read his eyes out of repair,
And groped his way up here, where we
Became acquainted, and where he
Met one of our girl-teachers, and,
If you 'll believe me, asked her hand
In marriage, though the girl was blind
As I am—and the girl *declined.*
Odd, was n't it? Look, you can see
Him waiting there. Fine, is n't he?
And handsome, eloquently wide
And high of brow, and dignified
With every outward grace, his sight
Restored to him, clear and bright
As day-dawn; waiting, waiting still
For the blind girl that never will
Be wife of his. How do I know?
You will recall a while ago
I told you he and I were friends.
In all that friendship comprehends,

I *was* his friend, I swear! why now,
Remembering his love, and how
His confidence was all my own,
I hear, in fancy, the low tone
Of his deep voice, so full of pride
And passion, yet so pacified
With his affliction, that it seems
An utterance sent out of dreams
Of saddest melody, withal
So sorrowfully musical
It was, and is, must ever be—
But I 'm digressing, pardon me.
I knew not anything of love
In those days, but of that above
All worldly passion,—for my art—
Music,—and that, with all my heart
And soul, blent in a love too great
For words of mine to estimate.
And though among my pupils she
Whose love my friend sought came to me
I only knew her fingers' touch
Because they loitered overmuch
In simple scales, and needs must be
Untangled almost constantly.
But she was bright In other ways,
And quick of thought; with ready plays

Of wit, and with a voice as sweet
To listen to as one might meet
In any oratorio—
And once I gravely told her so,—
And, at my words, her limpid tone
Of laughter faltered to a moan,
And fell from that into a sigh
That quavered all so wearily,
That I, without the tear that crept
Between the keys, had known she wept;
And yet the hand I reached for then
She caught away, and laughed again.
And when that evening I strolled
With my old friend, I, smiling, told
Him I believed the girl and he
Were matched and mated perfectly:
He was so noble; she, so fair
Of speech, and womanly of air;
He, strong, ambitious; she, as mild
And artless even as a child;
And with a nature, I was sure,
As worshipful as it was pure
And sweet, and brimmed with tender things
Beyond his rarest fancyings.
He stopped me solemnly. He knew,
He said, how good, and just, and true

Was all I said of her; but as
For his own virtues, let them pass,
Since they were nothing to the one
That he had set his heart upon;
For but that morning she had turned
Forever from him. Then I learned
That for a month he had delayed
His going from us, with no aid
Of hope to hold him,—meeting still
Her ever firm denial, till
Not even in his new-found sight
He found one comfort or delight.
And as his voice broke there, I felt
The brother-heart within me melt
In warm compassion for his own
That throbbed so utterly alone.
And then a sudden fancy hit
Along my brain; and coupling it
With a belief that I, indeed,
Might help my friend in his great need,
I warmly said that I would go
Myself, if he decided so,
And see her for him—that I knew
My pleadings would be listened to
Most seriously, and that she
Should love him, listening to me.

Go; bless me! And that was the last—
The last time his warm hand shut fast
Within my own—so empty since,
That the remembered finger-prints
I've kissed a thousand times, and wet
Them with the tears of all regret!

I know not how to rightly tell
How fared my quest, and what befell
Me, coming in the presence of
That blind girl, and her blinder love.
I know but little else than that
Above the chair in which she sat
I leant—reached for, and found her hand,
And held it for a moment, and
Took up the other—held them both—
As might a friend, I will take oath:
Spoke leisurely, as might a man
Praying for no thing other than
He thinks Heaven's justice:—She was blind,
I said, and yet a noble mind
Most truly loved her; one whose fond
Clear-sighted vision looked beyond
The bounds of her infirmity,
And saw the woman, perfectly
Modeled, and wrought out pure and true
And lovable. She quailed, and drew

Her hands away, but closer still
I caught them. "Rack me as you will!"
She cried out sharply—"Call me 'blind'—
Love ever is—I am resigned!
Blind is your friend; as blind as he
Am I—but blindest of the three—
Yea, blind as death—you will not see
My love for you is killing me!"

There is a memory that may
Not ever wholly fade away
From out my heart, so bright and fair
The light of it still glimmers there.
Why, it did seem as though my sight
Flamed back upon me, dazzling white
And godlike. Not one other word
Of hers I listened for or heard,
But I *saw* songs sung in her eyes
Till they did swoon up drowning-wise,
As my mad lips did strike her own
And we flashed one and one alone!
Ah! was it treachery for me
To kneel there, drinking eagerly
That torrent-flow of words that swept
Out laughingly the tears she wept?—

Sweet words! O sweeter far, maybe,
Than light of day to those that see,—
God knows, who did the rapture send
To me, and hold it from my friend.

And we were married half a year
Ago,—and he is—waiting here,
Heedless of that—or anything,
But just that he is lingering
To say good-bye to her, and bow—
As you may see him doing now,—
For there's her footstep in the hall ;
God bless her!—help him!—save us all !

RIGHT HERE AT HOME.

RIGHT here at home, boys, in old Hoosierdom,
  Where strangers allus joke us when they come,
And brag o' *their* old States and interprize—
Yit *settle* here; and 'fore they realize,
They 're "hoosier" as the rest of us, and live
Right here at home, boys, with their past fergive'!

Right here at home, boys, is the place, I guess,
Fer me and you and plain old happiness:
We hear the World 's lots grander—likely so,—
We 'll take the World 's word fer it and not go.—
We know *its* ways aint *our* ways—so we 'll stay
Right here at home, boys, where we *know* the way.

Right here at home, boys, where a well-to-do
Man 's plenty rich enough—and knows it, too,
And 's got a' extry dollar, any time,
To boost a feller up 'at *wants* to climb
And 's got the git-up in him to go in
And *git there*, like he purt'-nigh allus kin!

Right here at home, boys, is the place fer us!—
Where folks' heart 's bigger 'n their money-pu's';
And where a *common* feller 's jes as good
As ary other in the neighberhood:
The World at large don't worry you and me
Right here at home, boys, where we ort to be!

Right here at home, boys—jes right where we air!—
Birds do n't sing any sweeter anywhere:
Grass do n't grow any greener 'n she grows
Acrost the pastur' where the old path goes,—
All things in ear-shot 's purty, er in sight,
Right here at home, boys, ef we *size* 'em right.

Right here at home, boys, where the old home-place
Is sacerd to us as our mother's face,
Jes as we rickollect her, last she smiled
And kissed us—dyin' so and rickonciled,
Seein' us all at home here—none astray—
Right here at home, boys, where she sleeps to-day.

THE LITTLE FAT DOCTOR.

HE seemed so strange to me, every way—
  In manner, and form, and size,
From the boy I knew but yesterday,—
  I could hardly believe my eyes!

To hear his name called over there,
  My memory thrilled with glee
And leaped to picture him young and fair
  In youth, as he used to be.

But looking, only as glad eyes can,
  For the boy I knew of yore,
I smiled on a portly little man
  I had never seen before!—

Grave as a judge in courtliness—
  Professor-like and bland—
A little fat doctor and nothing less,
  With his hat in his kimboed hand.

But how we talked old times, and "chaffed"
  Each other with "Minnie" and "Jim"—
And how the little fat doctor laughed,
  And how I laughed with him!

"And it's pleasant," I thought, "though I yearn
      to see
  The face of the youth that was,
To know no boy could smile on me
  As the little fat doctor does!"

THE SHOEMAKER.

THOU Poet, who, like any lark,
 Dost whet thy beak and trill
From misty morn till murky dark,
 Nor ever pipe thy fill:
Hast thou not, in thy cheery note,
 One poor chirp to confer—
One verseful twitter to devote
 Unto the Shoe-ma-ker?

At early dawn he doth peg in
 His noble work and brave;
And eke from cark and wordly sin
 He seeketh soles to save;
And all day long, with quip and song,
 Thus stitcheth he the way
Our feet may know the right from wrong,
 Nor ever go a stray.

Soak kip in mind the Shoe-ma-ker,
 Nor slight his lasting fame:
Alway he waxeth tenderer
 In warmth of our acclaim;—
Aye, more than any artisan
 We glory in his art
Who ne'er, to help the under man,
 Neglects the upper part.

But toe the mark for him, and heel
   Respond to thee in kine—
Or kid—or calf, shouldst thou reveal
   A taste so superfine:
Thus let him jest—join in his laugh—
   Draw on his stock, and be
A shoer'd there's no rival half-
   Sole liberal as he.

Then, Poet, hail the Shoe-ma-ker
   For all his goodly deeds,—
Yea, bless him free for booting thee-
   The first of all thy needs!
And when at last his eyes grow dim,
   And nerveless drops his clamp,
In golden shoon pray think of him
   Upon his latest tramp.

THE OLD RETIRED SEA CAPTAIN.

THE old sea captain has sailed the seas
   So long, that the waves at mirth,
Or the waves gone wild, and the crests of these,
   Were as near playmates from birth :
He has loved both the storm and the calm, because
   They seemed as his brothers twain,—
The flapping sail was his soul's applause,
   And his rapture, the roaring main.

But now—like a battered hulk seems he,
   Cast high on a foreign strand,
Though he feels "in port," as it need must be,
   And the stay of a daughter's hand—
Yet ever the round of the listless hours,—
   His pipe, in the languid air—
The grass, the trees, and the garden flowers,
   And the strange earth everywhere !

And so betimes he is restless here
   In this little inland town,
With never a wing in the atmosphere
   But the wind-mill's, up and down ;
His daughter's home in this peaceful vale,
   And his grandchild 'twixt his knees—
But never the hail of a passing sail,
   Nor the surge of the angry seas !

He quits his pipe, and he snaps its neck—
    Would speak, though he coughs instead,
Then paces the porch like a quarter-deck
    With a reeling mast o'erhead!
Ho! the old sea captain's cheeks glow warm,
    And his eyes gleam grim and weird,
As he mutters about, like a thunder-storm,
    In the cloud of his beetling beard.

ROBERT BURNS WILSON.

WHAT intuition named thee?—Through what
     thrill
  Of the awed soul came the command divine
  Into the mother-heart, foretelling thine
Should palpitate with his whose raptures will
Sing on while daisies bloom and lavrocks trill
    Their undulating ways up through the fine
    Fair mists of heavenly reaches? Thy pure line
Falls as the dew of anthems, quiring still
The sweeter since the Scottish singer raised
    His voice therein, and, quit of every stress
      Of earthly ache and longing and despair,
Knew certainly each simple thing he praised
    Was no less worthy, for its lowliness,
      Than any joy of all the glory There.

TO THE SERENADER.

TINKLE on, O sweet guitar,
    Let the dancing fingers
Loiter where the low notes are
    Blended with the singer's:
Let the midnight pour the moon's
    Mellow wine of glory
Down upon him through the tune's
    Old romantic story!

I am listening, my love,
    Through the cautious lattice,
Wondering why the stars above
    All are blinking at us;
Wondering if his eyes from there
    Catch the moonbeam's shimmer
As it lights the robe I wear
    With a ghostly glimmer.

Lilt thy song, and lute away
    In the wildest fashion :—
Pour thy rippling roundelay
    O'er the heights of passion !—
Flash it down the fretted strings
    Till thy mad lips, missing
All but smothered whisperings,
    Press this rose I 'm kissing.

THE WIFE-BLESSÉD.

I.

IN youth he wrought, with eyes ablur,
  Lorn-faced and long of hair—
In youth—in youth he painted her
  A sister of the air—
Could clasp her not, but felt the stir
  Of pinions everywhere.

II.

She lured his gaze, in braver days,
  And tranced him sirenwise;
And he did paint her, through a haze
  Of sullen paradise,
With scars of kisses on her face
  And embers in her eyes.

III.

And now—nor dream nor wild conceit—
  Though faltering, as before—
Through tears he paints her, as is meet,
  Tracing the dear face o'er
With lilied patience meek and sweet
  As Mother Mary wore.

SISTER JONES'S CONFESSION.

I THOUGHT the deacon liked me, yit
   I warn't adzackly shore of it—
Fer, mind ye, time and time agin,
When jiners 'ud be comin' in,
I'd seed him shakin' hands as free
With all the sistern as with me!
But jurin' last Revival, where
He called on *me* to lead in prayer,
An' kneeled there with me, side by side,
A-whisper'n' "he felt sanctified
Jes' tetchin of my gyarment's hem,"—
That settled things as fur as them-
Thare *other* wimmin was concerned!—
And—well!—I know I must a-turned
A dozen colors!—*Flurried?—la!—*
No mortal sinner never saw
A gladder widder than the one
A-kneelin' there and wonderun'
Who'd pray!—So glad, upon my word,
I railly could n't thank the Lord!

THE CURSE OF THE WANDERING FOOT.

A LL hope of rest withdrawn me?—
   What dread command hath put
This awful curse upon me—
   The curse of the wandering foot!
Forward and backward and thither,
   And hither and yon again—
Wandering ever! And whither?
   Answer them, God! Amen.

The blue skies are far o'er me—
   The bleak fields near below:
Where the mother that bore me?—
   Where her grave in the snow?—
Glad in her trough of a coffin—
   The sad eyes frozen shut
That wept so often, often,
   The curse of the wandering foot!

Here in your marts I care not
   Whatsoever ye think.
Good folk many who dare not
   Give me to eat and drink:
Give me to sup of your pity—
   Feast me on prayers!—O ye,
Met I your Christ in the city
   He would fare forth with me—

Forward and onward and thither,
  And hither again and yon,
With milk for our drink together
  And honey to feed upon—
Nor hope of rest withdrawn us,
  Since the one Father put
The blesséd curse upon us—
  The curse of the wandering foot.

A MONUMENT FOR THE SOLDIERS.

A MONUMENT for the Soldiers!
   And what will ye build it of?
Can ye build it of marble, or brass, or bronze,
   Outlasting the Soldiers' love?
Can ye glorify it with legends
   As grand as their blood hath writ
From the inmost shrine of this land of thine
   To the outermost verge of it?

And the answer came: We would build it
   Out of our hopes made sure,
And out of our purest prayers and tears,
   And out of our faith secure:
We would build it out of the great white truths
   Their death hath sanctified,
And the sculptured forms of the men in arms,
   And their faces ere they died.

And what heroic figures
   Can the sculptor carve in stone?
Can the marble breast be made to bleed,
   And the marble lips to moan?
Can the marble brow be fevered?
   And the marble eyes be graved
To look their last, as the flag floats past,
   On the country they have saved?

And the answer came : The figures
  Shall all be fair and brave,
And, as befitting, as pure and white
  As the stars above their grave !
The marble lips, and breast and brow
  Whereon the laurel lies,
Bequeath us right to guard the flight
  Of the old flag in the skies !

A monument for the Soldiers !
  Built of a people's love,
And blazoned and decked and panoplied
  With the hearts ye build it of !
And see that ye build it stately,
  In pillar and niche and gate,
And high in pose as the souls of those
  It would commemorate !

THE RIVAL.

I SO loved once, when Death came by I hid
   Away my face,
And all my sweetheart's tresses she undid
    To make my hiding-place.

The dread shade passed me thus unheeding; and
    I turned me then
To calm my love—kiss down her shielding hand
    And comfort her again.

And lo! she answered not: And she did sit
    All fixedly,
With her fair face and the sweet smile of it,
    In love with Death, not me.

IRY AND BILLY AND JO.

IRY an' Billy an' Jo!—
    Iry an' Billy 's *the boys,*
An' *Jo's* their *dog,* you know,—
Their pictur 's took all in a row.
      Bet they kin kick up a noise—
      Iry and Billy, the boys,
And that-air little dog Jo!

Iry's the one 'at stands
    Up there a-lookin' so mild
An' meek—with his hat in his hands,
    Like such a *'bediant* child—
(*Sakes-alive!*)—An' *Billy* he sets
In the cheer an' holds onto Jo an' *sweats*
Hisse'f, a-lookin' so good! Ho-ho!
    Iry an' Billy an' Jo!

Yit the way them boys, you know,
    Usen to jes turn in
An' fight over that dog Jo
    Wuz a burnin'-shame-an'-a-sin!—

Iry *he'd* argy 'at, by gee-whizz!
That-air little Jo-dog wuz *his!*—
An' Billy *he'd* claim it wuzn't so—
'Cause the dog wuz *his'n*! —An' at it they'd go
Nip-an'-tugg, tooth-an'-toenail, you know—
    Iry an' Billy an' Jo!

But their Pa—(He wuz the marshal then)·
   He 'tended-like 'at he *jerked 'em up;*
An' got a jury o' Brickyard men
   An' helt *a trial* about the pup:
An' *he* says *he* jes like to a-died
When the rest o' us town-boys *testified*—
      Regardin', you know,
      Iry an' Billy an' Jo.—

'Cause we all knowed, when *the Gypsies* they
   Camped down here by the crick last Fall,
They brung Jo with 'em, an' give him away
   To Iry an' Billy fer nothin' at all!—
So the jury fetched in the *verdick* so
      Jo he ain't *neether* o' theirn fer *shore*—
      He's *both* their dog, an' jes no more!
      An' so
      They've quit quarrelin' long ago,
      Iry an' Billy an' Jo.

A WRAITH OF SUMMERTIME.

IN its color, shade and shine,
   'T was a summer warm as wine,
With an effervescent flavoring of flowered
      bough and vine,
And a fragrance and a taste
Of ripe roses gone to waste,
And a dreamy sense of sun- and moon- and
      star-light interlaced.

'T was a summer such as broods
O'er enchanted solitudes,
Where the hand of Fancy leads us through
      voluptuary moods,
And with lavish love out-pours
All the wea'th of out-of-doors,
And woos our feet o'er velvet paths and
      honeysuckle floors.

'T was a summertime long dead,—
And its roses, white and red,
And its reeds and water-lilies down along
      the river-bed,—
O they all are ghostly things—
For the ripple never sings,
And the rocking lily never even rustles as
      it rings!

HER BEAUTIFUL EYES.

O HER beautiful eyes! they are as blue as the dew
 On the violet's bloom when the morning is new,
And the light of their love is the gleam of the sun
O'er the meadows of Spring where the quick shadows
  run :
As the morn shifts the mists and the clouds from the
  skies—
So I stand in the dawn of her beautiful eyes.

And her beautiful eyes are as midday to me,
When the lily-bell bends with the weight of the bee,
And the throat of the thrush is a-pulse in the heat,
And the senses are drugged with the subtle and sweet
And delirious breaths of the air's lullabies—
So I swoon in the noon of her beautiful eyes.

O her beautiful eyes! they have smitten mine own
As a glory glanced down from the glare of The Throne;
And I reel, and I falter and fall, as afar
Fell the shepherds that looked on the mystical Star,
And yet dazed in the tidings that bade them arise—
So I grope through the night of her beautiful eyes.

DOT LEEDLE BOY.

OT 'S a leedle Ghristmas story
    Dot I told der leedle folks—
Und I vant you stop dot laughin'
    Und grackin' funny jokes!—
So-help me Peter-Moses!
    Ot 's no time for monkeyshine',
Ober I vas told you somedings
    Of dot leedle boy of mine!

Ot vas von cold Vinter vedder,
    Ven der snow vas all about—
Dot you have to chop der hatchet
    Eef you got der saur kraut!
Und der cheekens on der hind-leg
    Vas standin' in der shine
Der sun shmile out dot morning
    On dot leedle boy of mine.

He vas yoost a leedle baby
    Not bigger as a doll
Dot time I got acquaintet—
    Ach! you ought to heard 'im squall!—
I grackys! dot 's der moosic
    Ot make me feel so fine
Ven first I vas been marriet—
    Oh, dot leedle boy of mine!

He look' yoost like his fader!—
    So, ven der vimmen said
"Vot a purty leedle baby!"
    Katrina shake der head. . . .
I dink she must a-notice
    Dot der baby vas a-gryin',
Und she cover up der blankets
    Of dot leedle boy of mine.

Vel, ven he vas got bigger,
    Dot he grawl und bump his nose,
Und make der table over,
    Und molasses on his glothes—
Dot make 'im all der sveeter,—
    So I say to my Katrine
"Better you vas quit a-shpankin'
    Dot leedle boy of mine!"

I vish you could a-seen id—
    Ven he glimb up on der chair
Und shmash der lookin'glasses
    Ven he try to comb his hair
Mit a hammer!—Und Katrina
    Say "Dot's an ugly sign!"
But I laugh und vink my fingers
    At dot leedle boy of mine.

But vonce, dot Vinter morning,
  He shlip out in der snow
Mitout no stockin's on 'im.—
  He say he "vant to go
Und fly some mit der birdies!"
  Und ve give 'im medi-cine
Ven he catch der "parrygoric"—
  Dot leedle boy of mine!

Und so I set und nurse 'im,
  Vile der Ghristmas vas come roun',
Und I told 'im 'bout "Kriss Kringle,"
  How he come der chimbly down:
Und I ask 'im eef he love 'im
  Eef he bring 'im someding fine?
"Nicht besser as mein fader,"
  Say dot leedle boy of mine.—

Und he put his arms aroun' me
  Und hug so close und tight,
I hear der gclock a-tickin'
  All der balance of der night! . . .
Someding make me feel so funny
  Ven I say to my Katrine
"Let us go und fill der stockin's
  Of dot leedle boy of mine."

Vell.—Ve buyed a leedle horses
  Dot you pull 'im mit a shtring,
Und a leedle fancy jay-bird—
  Eef you vant to hear 'im sing
You took 'im by der top-knot
  Und yoost blow in behine—
Und dot make much *spectakel*—
  For dot leedle boy of mine!

Und gandles, nuts and raizens—
  Unt I buy a leedle drum
Dot I vant to hear 'im rattle
  Ven der Gristmas morning come!
Und a leedle shmall tin rooster
  Dot vould crow so loud und fine
Ven he sqveeze 'im in der morning,
  Dot leedle boy of mine!

Und—vile ve vas a-fixin'—
  Dot leedle boy vake out!
I t'ought he been a-dreamin'
  "Kriss Kringle" vas about,—
For he say—"*Dot's him!—I see 'im*
  Mit der shtars dot make der shine!"
Und he yoost keep on a-gryin'—
  Dot leedle boy of mine,—

Und gottin' vorse und vorser—
    Und tumble on der bed!
So—ven der doctor seen id,
    He kindo' shake his head,
Und feel his pulse—und visper
    "Der boy is a-dyin'."
You dink I could *believe* id?—
    Dot leedle boy of mine?

I told you, friends—dot's someding,
    Der last time dot he speak
Und say "*Goot-bye, Kriss Kringle!*"
    —Dot make me feel so veak
I yoost kneel down und drimble,
    Und bur-sed out a-gryin'
"*Mein Gott, mein Gott im Himmel!—*
    Dot leedle boy of mine!"

       *   *   *   *   *   *

Der sun do n't shine *dot* Gristmas!
    . . . Eef dot leedle boy vould *liff'd*—
No deefer-en'! for *Heaven* vas
    His leedle Gristmas-gift! . . .
Und der *rooster*, und der *gandy*,
    Und me—und my Katrine—
Und der jay-bird—is a-vaiting
    For dot leedle boy of mine.

DONN PIATT OF MAC-O-CHEE.

I.

DONN Piatt—of Mac-o-chee,—
    Not the one of History,
Who, with flaming tongue and pen,
Scathes the vanities of men;
Not the one whose biting wit
Cuts pretense and etches it
On the brazen brow that dares
Filch the laurel that it wears:
Not the Donn Piatt whose praise
Echoes in the noisy ways
Of the faction, onward led
By the statesman !—But, instead,
Give the simple man to me,—
Donn Piatt of Mac-o-chee!

II.

Donn Piatt of Mac-o-chee!
Branches of the old oak tree,
Drape him royally in fine
Purple shade and golden shine!

Emerald plush of sloping lawn
Be the throne he sits upon!
And, O Summer sunset, thou
Be his crown, and gild a brow
Softly smoothed and soothed and calmed
By the breezes, mellow-palmed
As Erata's white hand agleam
On the forehead of a dream.—
So forever rule o'er me,
Donn Piatt of Mac-o-chee!

III.

Donn Piatt of Mac-o-chee:
Through a lilied memory
Plays the wayward little creek
Round thy home at hide-and-seek—
As I see and hear it, still
Romping round the wooded hill,
Till its laugh-and-babble blends
With the silence while it sends
Glances back to kiss the sight,
In its babyish delight,
Ere it strays amid the gloom
Of the glens that burst in bloom
Of the rarest rhyme for thee,
Donn Piatt of Mac-o-chee!

IV.

Donn Piatt of Mac-o-chee!
What a darling destiny
Has been mine—to meet him there—
Lolling in an easy chair
On the terrace, while he told
Reminiscences of old—
Letting my cigar die out,
Hearing poems talked about;
And entranced to hear him say
Gentle things of Thackeray,
Dickens, Hawthorne, and the rest,
Known to him as host and guest—
Known to him as he to me—
Donn Piatt of Mac-o-chee!

THEM FLOWERS.

TAKE a feller 'at's sick and laid up on the shelf,
  All shaky, and ga'nted, and pore—
Jes all so knocked out he can't handle hisself
  With a stiff upper-lip any more;
Shet him up all alone in the gloom of a room
  As dark as the tomb, and as grim,
And then take and send him some roses in bloom,
  And you can have fun out o' him!

You've ketched him 'fore now—when his liver
        was sound
  And his appetite notched like a saw—
A-mockin' you, mayby, fer romancin' round
  With a big posy-bunch in yer paw;
But you ketch him, say, when his health is away,
  And he's flat on his back in distress,
And *then* you kin trot out yer little bokay
  And not be insulted, I guess!

You see, it's like this, what his weaknesses is,—
  Them flowers makes him think of the days
Of his innocent youth, and that mother o' his,
  And the roses that *she* us't to raise:—

So here, all alone with the roses you send—
    Bein' sick and all trimbly and faint,—
My eyes is—my eyes is—my eyes is—old friend—
    Is a-leakin'—I 'm blamed ef they ain't!

THE QUIET LODGER.

THE man that rooms next door to me:
 Two weeks ago, this very night,
He took possession quietly,
 As any other lodger might—
  But why the room next mine should so
  Attract him I was vexed to know,—
  Because his quietude, in fine,
  Was far superior to mine.

"Now, I like quiet, truth to tell,
 A tranquil life is sweet to me—
But *this*," I sneered, "suits me too well.—
 He shuts his door so noiselessly,
  And glides about so very mute,
  In each mysterious pursuit,
  His silence is oppressive, and
  Too deep for me to understand."

Sometimes, forgetting book or pen,
 I 've found my head in breathless poise
Lifted, and dropped in shame again,
 Hearing some alien ghost of noise—
  Some smothered sound that seemed to be
  A trunk-lid dropped unguardedly,
  Or the crisp writhings of some quire
  Of manuscript thrust in the fire.

Then I have climbed, and closed in vain
  My transom, opening in the hall;
Or close against the window-pane
  Have pressed my fevered face,—but all
    The day or night without held not
    A sight or sound or counter-thought
    To set my mind one instant free
    Of this man's silent mastery.

And often I have paced the floor
  With muttering anger, far at night,
Hearing, and cursing, o'er and o'er,
  The muffled noises, and the light
    And tireless movements of this guest
    Whose silence raged above my rest
    Hoarser than howling storms at sea—
    The man that rooms next door to me.

But twice or thrice, upon the stair,
  I've seen his face—most strangely wan,—
Each time upon me unaware
  He came—smooth'd past me, and was gone.—
    So like a whisper he went by,
    I listened after, ear and eye,
    Nor could my chafing fancy tell
    The meaning of one syllable.

Last night I caught him, face to face,—
  He entering his room, and I
Glaring from mine: He paused a space
  And met my scowl all shrinkingly,
    But with full gentleness: The key
    Turned in his door—and I could see
    It tremblingly withdrawn and put
    Inside, and then—the door was shut.

Then silence. *Silence!*—why, last night
  The silence was tumultuous,
And thundered on till broad daylight;—
  O never has it stunned me thus!—
    It rolls, and moans, and mumbles yet.—
    Ah, God! how loud may silence get
    When man mocks at a brother man
    Who answers but as silence can!

The silence grew, and grew, and grew,
  Till at high noon to-day 't was heard
Throughout the house; and men flocked through
  The echoing halls, with faces blurred
    With pallor, gloom, and fear, and awe,
    And shuddering at what they saw—
    The quiet lodger, as he lay
    Stark of the life he cast away.

  *   *   *   *   *   *   *

So strange to-night—those voices there,
　Where all so quiet was before:
They say the face has not a care
　Nor sorrow in it any more—
　　His latest scrawl:—"Forgive me—You
　　Who prayed, 'they know not what they do!'"
　　My tears will never let me see
　　This man that rooms next door to me!

THE WATCHES OF THE NIGHT.

O THE waiting in the watches of the night!
  In the darkness, desolation, and contrition and
      affright;
The awful hush that holds us shut away from all
      delight :
  The ever weary memory that ever weary goes
  Recounting ever over every aching loss it knows—
  The ever weary eyelids gasping ever foi repose—
      In the dreary, weary watches of the night !

Dark—stifling dark—the watches of the night !
With tingling nerves at tension, how the blackness
      flashes white
With spectral visitations smitten past the inner sight!—
  What shuddering sense of wrongs we've wrought
      that may not be redressed—
  Of tears we did not brush away—of lips we left
      unpressed,
  And hands that we let fall, with all their loyalty
      unguessed !
      Ah ! the empty, empty watches of the night !

What solace in the watches of the night?—
What frailest staff of hope to stay—what faintest shaft
    of light?
Do we *dream* and dare *believe* it, that by never weight
    of right
  Of our own poor weak deservings, we shall win the
    dawn at last—
  Our famished souls find freedom from this penance
    for the past,
  In a faith that leaps and lightens from the gloom
    that flees aghast—
    Shall we survive the watches of the night?

One leads us through the watches of the night—
By the ceaseless intercession of our loved ones lost to
    sight
He is with us through all trials, in His mercy and His
    might ;—
  With our mothers there about Him, all our sorrow
    disappears,
  Till the silence of our sobbing is the prayer the
    Master hears,
  And His hand is laid upon us with the tenderness of
    tears
    In the waning of the watches of the night.

HIS VIGIL.

CLOSE the book and dim the light,
    I shall read no more to-night.
No—I am not sleepy, dear—
Do not go: sit by me here
In the darkness and the deep
Silence of the watch I keep.
Something in your presence so
Soothes me—as in long ago
I first felt your hand—as now—
In the darkness touch my brow:
I've no other wish than you
Thus should fold mine eyelids to,
Saying nought of sigh or tear—
Just as God were sitting here.

THE PLAINT HUMAN

SEASON of snows, and season of flowers,
  Seasons of loss and gain!—
Since grief and joy must alike be ours,
  Why do we still complain?

Ever our failing, from sun to sun,
  O my intolerent brother:—
We want just a little too little of one,
  And much too much of the other.

BY ANY OTHER NAME.

FIRST the teacher called the roll,
     Clos't to the beginnin',
"Addeliney Bowersox!"
     Set the school a-grinnin'.
Wintertime, and stingin'-cold
     When the session took up—
Cold as *we* all looked at *her*,
     Though *she* couldn't look up!

Total stranger to us, too—
     Country-folks ain't allus
Nigh so shameful unpolite
     As some people call us!—
But the honest facts is, *then*,
     Addeliney Bower-
Sox's feelin's was so hurt
     She cried half an hour!

My dest was acrost from her'n:
     Set and watched her tryin'
To p'tend she didn't keer,
     And a kind o' dryin'
Up her tears with smiles—tel I
     Thought, "Well, ' *Addeliney*
Bowersox' is plain, but *she*'s
     Purty as a piney!"

It 's be'n many of a year
  Sence that most oncommon
Cur'ous name o' *Bowersox*
  Struck me so abomin-
Nubble and outlandish-like!—
  I changed it to Adde-
Liney *Daubenspeck*—and *that*
  Nearly killed her Daddy!

TO AN IMPORTUNATE GHOST.

GET gone, thou most uncomfortable ghost!
    Thou really dost annoy me with thy thin
  Impalpable transparency of grin;
And the vague, shadowy shape of thee almost
Hath vext me beyond boundary and coast
    Of my broad patience. Stay thy chattering chin,
    And reel the tauntings of thy vain tongue in,
Nor tempt me further with thy vaporish boast
    That I am *helpless* to combat thee! Well,
Have at thee, then! Yet if a doom most dire
    Thou wouldst escape, flee whilst thou canst!—Revile
Me not, Miasmic Mist!—Rank Air! *retire!*
    One instant longer an thou haunt'st me, I'll
Inhale thee, O thou wraith despicable!

THE QUARREL.

THEY faced each other: Topaz-brown
        And lambent burnt her eyes and shot
Sharp flame at his of amethyst.—
"I hate you! Go, and be forgot
    As death forgets!" their glitter *hissed*
(So *seemed* it) in their hatred. Ho!
Dared any mortal front her so?—
Tempestuous eyebrows knitted down—
Tense nostril, mouth—no muscle slack,—
And black—the suffocating black—
The stifling blackness of her frown!

Ah! but the lifted face of her!
And the twitched lip and tilted head!
Yet he did neither wince nor stir,—
Only—his hands clenched; and, instead
Of words, he answered with a stare
That stammered not in aught it said,
As might his voice if trusted there.

And what—what spake his steady gaze?—
Was there a look that harshly fell
To scoff her?—or a syllable
Of anger?—or the bitter phrase
That myrrhs the honey of love's lips,
Or curdles blood as poison drips?

What made their breasts to heave and swell
As billows under bows of ships
In broken seas on stormy days?
We may not know—nor *they* indeed—
What mercy found them in their need.

A sudden sunlight smote the gloom;
And round about them swept a breeze,
With faint breaths as of clover-bloom;
A bird was heard, through drone of bees,—
Then, far and clear and eerily,
A child's voice from an orchard-tree—
Then laughter, sweet as the perfume
Of lilacs, could the hearing see.
And he—O Love! he fed thy name
On bruiséd kisses, while her dim
Deep eyes, with all their inner flame,
Like drowning gems were turned on him.

THE OLD YEAR AND THE NEW.

I.

AS one in sorrow looks upon
  The dead face of a loyal friend,
By the dim light of New Year's dawn
  I saw the Old Year end.

Upon the pallid features lay
  The dear old smile—so warm and bright
Ere thus its cheer had died away
  In ashes of delight.

The hands that I had learned to love
  With strength of passion half divine,
Were folded now, all heedless of
  The emptiness of mine.

The eyes that once had shed their bright
  Sweet looks like sunshine, now were dull,
And ever lidded from the light
  That made them beautiful.

II.

The chimes of bells were in the air,
    And sounds of mirth in hall and street,
With pealing laughter everywhere
    And throb of dancing feet:

The mirth and the convivial din
    Of revelers in wanton glee,
With tunes of harp and violin
    In tangled harmony.

But with a sense of nameless dread,
    I turned me, from the merry face
Of this newcomer, to my dead;
    And, kneeling there a space,

I sobbed aloud, all tearfully:—
    By this dear face so fixed and cold,
O Lord, let not this New Year be
    As happy as the old!

THE HEREAFTER.

HEREAFTER! O we need not waste
Our smiles or tears, whate'er befall:
No happiness but holds a taste
Of something sweeter, after all;—
No depth of agony but feels
Some fragment of abiding trust,—
Whatever death unlocks or seals,
The mute beyond is just.

JOHN BROWN.

WRIT in between the lines of his life-deed
    We trace the sacred service of a heart
Answering the Divine command, in every part
Bearing on human weal: His love did feed
The loveless; and his gentle hands did lead
The blind, and lift the weak, and balm the smart
Of other wounds than rankled at the dart
In his own breast, that gloried thus to bleed.
He served the lowliest first—nay, them alone—
The most despiséd that e'er wreaked vain breath
In cries of suppliance in the reign whereat
Red Guilt sate squat upon her spattered throne.—
For these doomed there it was he went to death.
God! how the merest man loves one like that!

A CUP OF TEA.

I HAVE sipped, with drooping lashes,
  Dreamy draughts of Verzenay;
I have flourished brandy-smashes
  In the wildest sort of way;
I have joked with "Tom and Jerry"
  Till "wee hours ayont the twal' —
But I 've found my tea the very
  Safest tipple of them all!

'T is a mystical potation
  That exceeds in warmth of glow
And divine exhilaration
  All the drugs of long ago—
All of old magicians' potions—
  Of Medea's filtered spells—
Or of fabled isles and oceans
  Where the Lotos-eater dwells!

Though I 've reveled o'er late lunches
  With *blasé* dramatic stars,
And absorbed their wit and punches
  And the fumes of their cigars—
Drank in the latest story,
  With a cock-tail either end,—
I have drained a deeper glory
  In a cup of tea, my friend.

Green, Black, Moyune, Formosa,
  Congou, Amboy, Pingsuey—
No odds the name it knows—ah!
  Fill a cup of it for me!
And, as I clink my china
  Against your goblet's brim,
My tea in steam shall twine a
  Fragrant laurel round its rim.

JUDITH.

O HER eyes are amber-fine—
   Dark and deep as wells of wine,
While her smile is like the noon
Splendor of a day of June.
If she sorrow—lo! her face
It is like a flowery space
In bright meadows, overlaid
With light clouds and lulled with shade.
If she laugh—it is the trill
Of the wayward whippoorwill
Over upland pastures, heard
Echoed by the mocking-bird
In dim thickets dense with bloom
And blurred cloyings of perfume.
If she sigh—a zephyr swells
Over odorous asphodels
And wan lilies in lush plots
Of moon-drown'd forget-me-nots.
Then, the soft touch of her hand—
Takes all breath to understand
What to liken it thereto!—
Never roseleaf rinsed with dew
Might slip soother-suave than slips
Her slow palm, the while her lips
Swoon through mine, with kiss on kiss
Sweet as heated honey is.

THE ARTEMUS OF MICHIGAN.

GRAND HAVEN is in Michigan, and in possession,
        too,
Of as many rare attractions as our party ever knew:—
The fine hotel, the landlord, and the lordly bill of fare,
And the dainty-neat completeness of the pretty waiters
        there;
The touch on the piano in the parlor, and the trill
Of the exquisite soprano, in our fancy singing still;
Our cozy room, its comfort, and our thousand grateful
        tho'ts,
And at our door the gentle face
        Of
                H.
                        Y.
                                Potts!

His artless observations, and his drollery of style,
Bewildered with that sorrowful serenity of smile—
The eye's elusive twinkle, and the twitching of the lid,
Like he didn't go to say it and was sorry that he did.
O Artemus of Michigan! so worthy of the name,
Our manager indorses it, and Bill Nye does the same—
You tickled our affection in so many tender spots
That even Recollection laughs
        At
                H.
                        Y.
                                Potts!

And hark ye! O Grand Haven! count your rare
    attractions o'er—

The commerce of your ships at sea, and ships along
    the shore ;

Your railroads, and your industries, and interests untold,

Your Opera House—our lecture, and the gate-receipts in
    gold !—

Ay, Banner Town of Michigan ! count all your treasures
    through—

Your crowds of summer tourists, and your Sanita-
    rium, too;

Your lake, your beach, your drives, your breezy groves
    and grassy plots,

But head the list of all of these
        With
            H.
                Y.
                    Potts !

THE HOODOO.

OWNED a pair o' skates onc't.—Traded
    Fer 'em,—stropped 'em on and waded
Up and down the crick, a-waitin'
Tel she 'd freeze up fit fer skatin'.
Mildest winter I remember—
    More like Spring- than Winter-weather!—
Did n't *frost* tel bout December—
    Git up airly ketch a feather
Of it, mayby, 'crost the winder—
Sunshine swinge it like a cinder!

Well—I *waited*—and *kep'* waitin'!
    Couldn't see my money's w'oth in
Them-air skates and was no skatin'
    Ner no hint o' ice ner nothin'!
So, one day—along in airly
Spring—I swopped 'em off—and barely
Closed the dicker, 'fore the weather
    Natchurly jes slipped the ratchet,
And crick—tail-race—all together,
    Froze so tight cat couldn't scratch it!

THE RIVALS; OR THE SHOWMAN'S RUSE

A TRAGI-COMEDY, IN ONE ACT.

PERSONS REPRESENTED.

BILLY MILLER	}	The Rivals
JOHNNY WILLIAMS		
TOMMY WELLS		Conspirator

TIME—Noon: SCENE—Country Town—*Rear view of the Miller Mansion, showing Barn, with practical loft-window opening on alley-way, with colored-crayon poster beneath, announcing :—*"BILLY MILLER'S Big Show and Monstur Circus and Equareum! A shour-bath fer Each and All fer 20 pins. This Afternoon! Don't fer git the date!" *Enter* TOMMY WELLS *and* JOHNNY WILLIAMS, *who gaze awhile at poster,* TOMMY *secretly smiling and winking at* BILLY MILLER, *concealed at loft-window above.*

TOMMY (to JOHNNY).
>Guess 'at Billy haint got back,—
>Can 't see nothin' through the crack—
>Can 't hear nothin' neither—No !
>. . . Thinks he 's got the dandy show,
>Don't he?

JOHNNY (scornfully)—

   'Course! but what *I* care?—
   He haint got no show in there!—
   What's *he* got in there but that
   Old hen, cooped up with a cat
   An' a turkle, an' that thing
   'At he calls his "circus-ring?"
   "*What a circus-ring!*" I'd *quit!*
   Bet *mine's* twic't as big as it!

TOMMY—

   Yes, but *you* got no machine
   Wat you bathe with, painted green,
   With a string to work it, guess!

JOHNNY (contemptuously)—

   Folks don't *bathe* in *circuses!*—
   Ladies comes to *mine*, you bet!
   I' got seats where girls can set;
   An' a dressin'-room, an' all,
   Fixed up in my pony's stall!—
   Yes, an' I' got *carpet*, too,
   Fer the tumblers, and a blue
   Center-pole !

TOMMY—

> Well, Billy, he's
> Got a tight-rope an' trapeze,
> An' a hoop 'at he jumps through
> Head-first!

JOHNNY—

> Well, what's *that* to do—
> Lightin' on a pile o' hay?
> Haint no *actin'* thataway!

TOMMY—

> Don't care what you say, he draws
> Bigger crowds than you do, 'cause
> Sense he started up, I know
> All the fellers says his show
> Is the best-un!

JOHNNY—

> Yes, an' he
> Better not tell things on me!
> His old circus haint no good!—
> 'Cause he's got the neighberhood
> Down on me he thinks 'at I'm
> Goin' to stand it all the time;
> Thinks ist 'cause my Pa don't 'low
> Me to fight, he's got me now.

An' can say I lie, an' call
Me ist anything at all!
Billy Miller thinks I am   ˙
'Feared to say 'at he says "dam"—
Yes, and *worser* ones! and I'm
Goin' to tell his folks sometime!—
An' ef he don't shet his head
I'll tell worse 'an *that* he said
When he fighted Willie King—
An' got licked like ever'thing!—
Billy Miller better shin
Down his Daddy's lane agin,
Like a cowardy-calf, an' climb
In fer home another time!
Better—

[*Here* BILLY *leaps down from the loft upon his unsuspecting victim; and two minutes later,* JOHNNY, *with the half of a straw hat, a bleeding nose, and a straight rent across one trouser-knee, makes his inglorious—exit.*]

WHAT CHRIS'MAS FETCHED THE WIGGINSES.

WINTERTIME, er Summertime,
    Of late years I notice I'm,
Kindo'-like, more subjec' to
What the *weather* is. Now, you
Folks 'at lives in town, I s'pose,
Thinks its bully when it snows;
But the chap 'at chops and hauls
Yer wood fer ye, and then stalls,
And snapps tuggs and swingletrees,
And then has to walk er freeze,
Haint so much "stuck on" the snow
As stuck *in* it—Bless ye, no!—
When its packed, and sleighin's good,
And *church* in the neighberhood,
Them 'at 's *got* their girls, I guess,
Takes 'em, likely, more er less.
Tell the plain facts o' the case,
No men-folks about our place
On'y me and Pap—and he
'Lows 'at young folks' company

Allus made him sick! So I
Jes don't want, and jes don't try!
Chinkypin, the dad-burn town,
'S too fur off to loaf aroun'
Either day er night—and no
Law compellin' me to go!—
'Less 'n some Old-Settlers' Day,
Er big-doin's thataway—
Then, to tell the p'inted fac',
I 've went more so 's to come back
By old Guthrie's 'still-house, where
Minors *has* got licker there—
That 's pervidin' we could show 'em
Old folks sent fer it from home!
Visit roun' the neighbers some,
When the *boys* wants me to come.—
Coon-hunt with 'em ; er set traps
Fer mussrats ; er jes, perhaps,
Lay in roun' the stove, you know,
And parch corn, and let her snow!
Mostly, nights like these, you 'll be
(Ef you' got a writ fer *me*)
Ap' to skeer me up, I guess,
In about the Wigginses.
Nothin' roun' *our* place to keep
Me at home—with Pap asleep

'Fore it 's dark; and Mother in
Mango pickles to her chin;
And the girls, all still as death,
Piecin' quilts.—Sence I drawed breath
Twenty year' ago, and heerd
Some girls whispern' so 's it 'peared
Like they had a row o' pins
In their mouth—right there begins
My first rickollections, built
On that-air blame old piece-quilt!

Summertime, it 's jes the same—
'Cause I 've noticed,—and I claim,
As I said afore, I 'm more
Subjec' to the weather, *shore*,
'Proachin' my majority,
Than I ever ust to be!
Callin' back *last* Summer, say,—
Don't seem hardly past away—
With night closin' in, and all
S' lonesome-like in the dew-fall:
Bats—ad-drat their ugly muggs!—
Flickern' by; and lightnin'-bugs
Huckstern' roun' the airly night
Little sickly gasps o' light;—
Whip-poor-wills, like all possess'd,
Moanin' out their mournfullest;—

Frogs and katydids and things
Jes *clubs* in and sings and sings
Their *ding-dangdest!*—Stock 's all fed,
And Pap 's washed his feet fer bed;—
Mother and the girls all down
At the milk-shed, foolin' roun'—
No wunder 'at I git blue,
And lite out—and so would you!
I caint stay aroun' no place
Whur they haint no livin' face:—
'Crost the fields and thue the gaps
Of the hills they 's friends, perhaps,
Waitin' somers, 'at kin be
Kindo' comfertin' to me!

Neighbers all is plenty good,
Scattered thue this neighberhood;
Yit, of all, I like to jes
Drap in on the Wigginses.—
Old man, and old lady too,
'Pear-like, makes so much o' you—
Least, they 've allus pampered me
Like one of the fambily.—
The boys, too, 's all thataway—
Want you jes to come and stay;—
Price, and Chape, and Mandaville,
Poke, Chasteen, and "Catfish Bill"—

Poke's the runt of all the rest,
But he's jes the beatinest
Little schemer, fer fourteen,
Anybody ever seen!—
"Like his namesake," old man claims,
"Jeems K. Poke, the first o' names!
Full o' tricks and jokes—and you
Never know what *Poke's* go' do!"
Genius, too, that-air boy is,
With them awk'ard hands o' his:
Gits this blame pokeberry-juice,
Er some stuff, fer ink—and goose-
Quill pen-p'ints: And then he'll draw
Dogdest pictures yevver saw!
Er make deers and eagles good
As a writin'-teacher could!
Then they's two twin boys they've riz
Of old Coonrod Wigginses
'At's deceast—and glad of it,
'Cause his widder's livin' yit!

Course *the boys* is mostly jes'
Why I go to Wigginses.—
Though *Melviney*, sometimes, *she*
Gits her slate and algebry
And jes' sets there ciphern' thue
Sums old Ray hisse'f caint do!—

Jes' sets there, and tilts her chair
Forreds tel, 'pear-like, her hair
Jes' *spills* in her lap—and then
She jes' dips it up again
With her hands, as white, I swan,
As the apern she's got on!

Talk o' hospitality!—
Go to Wigginses with me—
Overhet, or froze plum thue,
You'll find welcome waitin' you:—
Th'ow out yer tobacker 'fore
You set foot acrost that floor,—
"Got to eat whatever's set—
Got to drink whatever's wet!"
Old man's sentimuns—them's his—
And means jes the best they is!
Then he lights his pipe; and she,
The old lady, presen'ly
She lights her'n; and Chape and Poke.—
I haint got none, ner don't smoke,—
(In the crick afore their door—
Sorto so's 'at I'd be shore—
Drownded mine one night and says
"I won't smoke at *Wigginses!*")
Price he's mostly talkin' 'bout
Politics, and "thieves turned out"—

What he's go' to be, ef he
Ever "gits there"—and "we'll see!"—
Poke he 'lows they's blame few men
Go' to hold their breath tel then!
Then Melviney smiles, as she
Goes on with her algebry,
And the clouds clear, and the room's
Sweeter 'n crabapple-blooms!
(That Melviney, she' got some
Most surprisin' ways, I gum!—
Don't 'pear like she ever *says*
Nothin', yit you'll *listen* jes
Like she *was* a-talkin', and
Half-way seem to understand,
But not quite,—*Poke* does, I know,
'Cause he good as told me so,—
Poke's her favo-rite; and he—
That is, confidentially—
He's *my* favo-rite—and I
Got my whurfore and my why!)

I haint never ben no hand
Much at talkin', understand,
But they's *thoughts* o' mine 'at 's jes
Jealous o' them Wigginses!—
Gift o' talkin 's what they' got,
Whether they want to er not.—

F'r instunce, start the old man on
Huntin'-scrapes, 'fore game was gone,
'Way back in the Forties, when
Bears stold pigs right out the pen,
Er went waltzin' 'crost the farm
With a bee-hive on their arm!—
And—sir, *ping!* the old man's gun
Has plumped over many a one,
Firin' at him from afore
That-air very cabin-door!
Yes—and *painters*, prowlin' 'bout,
Allus darkest nights.—Lay out
Clost yer cattle.—Great, big red
Eyes a-blazin' in their head,
Glittern' 'long the timber-line—
Shine out some, and then *un*-shine,
And shine back—Then, stiddy! whizz!
'N there yer Mr. Painter is
With a hole bored spang between
Them-air eyes! Er start Chasteen,
Say, on blooded racin'-stock,
Ef you want to hear him talk;
Er tobacker—how to raise,
Store, and k-yore it, so's she pays:
The old lady—and she'll cote
Scriptur' tel she'll git yer vote!

Prove to you 'at wrong is right,
Jes as plain as black is white:
Prove when you 're asleep in bed
You 're a-standin' on yer head,
And yer train 'at 's goin' West,
'S goin' East its level best;
And when bees dies, it 's their wings
Wears out—and a thousand things!
And the boys is "chips," you know,
"Off the old block"—So I go
To the Wigginses, 'cause—jes
'Cause I *like* the Wigginses—
Even ef Melviney *she*
Hardly 'pears to notice me!

Rid to Chinkypin this week—
Yisterd'y.—No snow to speak
Of, and didn't have no sleigh
Anyhow; so, as I say,
I rid in—and froze one ear
And both heels—and I don't keer!—
"Mother and the girls kin jes
Bother 'bout their Chris'mases
Next time fer *theirse'vs*, I jack!"
Thinks-says-I, a-startin' back,—
Whole durn meal-bag full of things
Wropped in paper-sacks, and strings

Liable to snap their holt
Jes at any little jolt!
That in front o' me, and *wind*
With *nicks* in it, 'at jes skinned
Me alive!—I'm here to say
Nine mile' hossback thataway
Would a-walked my log! But, as
Somepin' allus comes to pass,
As I topped old Guthrie's hill,
Saw a buggy, front the 'Still,
P'inted home'ards, and a thin
Little chap jes climbin' in.
Six more minutes I were there
On the groun's!—And course it were—
It were little Poke—and he
Nearly fainted to see me!—
"You ben in to Chinky, too?"
"Yes; and go' ride back with you,"
I-says-I. He he'pped me find
Room fer my things in behind—
Stript my hoss's reins down, and
Put his mitt' on the right hand
So's to lead—"Pile in!" says he,
"But you've struck pore company!"
Noticed he was pale—looked sick,
Kindo-like, and had a quick

Way o' flickin' them-air eyes
O' his roun' 'at didn't size
Up right with his usual style—
S' I, "You well?" He tried to smile,
But his chin shuck and tears come.—
"I 've run 'Viney 'way from home!"

Don't know jes what all occurred
Next ten seconds—Nary word,
But my heart jes drapt, stobbed thue,
And whirlt over and come to.—
Wrenched a big quart bottle from
That fool-boy!—and cut my thumb
On his little fiste-teeth—helt
Him snug in one arm, and felt
That-air little heart o' his
Churn the blood o' Wigginses
Into that old bead 'at spun
Roun' her, spilt at Lexington!
His k'niptions, like enough,
He'pped us both,—though it was rough—
Rough on him, and rougher on
Me when last his nerve was gone,
And he laid there still, his face
Fishin' fer some hidin'-place
Jes a leetle lower down
!n my breast than he'd yit foun'!

Last I kindo' soothed him, so 's
He could talk.—And what you s'pose
Them-air revelations of
Poke's was?... He 'd ben writin' love-
Letters to Melviney, and
Givin her to understand
They was from "a young man who
Loved her," and—"the violet 's blue
'N sugar 's sweet"—and Lord knows what!
Tel, 'peared-like, Melviney got
S' interested in "the young
Man," Poke *he* says, 'at she brung
A' answer onc't fer him to take,
Statin' "she 'd die fer his sake,"
And writ fifty xs "fer
Love-kisses fer him from her!"
I was standin' in the road
By the buggy, all I knowed
When Poke got that fer.—"That 's why,"
Poke says, "I 'fessed up the lie—
Had to—'cause I see," says he,
"'Viney was in airnest—she
Cried, too, when I told her.—Then
She swore me, and smiled again,
And got Pap and Mother to
Let me hitch and drive her thue

Into Chinkypin, to be
At Aunt 'Rindy's Chris'mas-tree—
That's to-night." Says I, "Poke—durn
Your lyin' soul!—'s that beau o' hern—
That—*she*—loves—Does *he* live in
That hellhole o' Chinkypin?"
"No," says Poke, " er 'Viney would
Went some *other* neighberhood."
"Who *is* the blame whelp?" says I.
"Promised 'Viney, hope I 'd die
Ef I ever told!" says Poke,
Pittiful and jes heart-broke—
"'Sides that 's why she left the place,—
'She caint look him in the face
Now no more on earth!' she says.—"
And the child broke down and jes
Sobbed! Says I, "Poke, I p'tend
T' be *your* friend, and your *Pap's* friend,
And your *Mother's* friend, and all
The *boys'* friend, little, large and small—
The *whole fambily's* friend—and you
Know that means *Melviney*, too.—
Now—you hush yer troublin'!—I'm
Go' to he'p friends ever' time—
On'y in *this* case, *you* got
To he'p *me*—and, like as not

I kin he'p Melviney then,
And we'll have her home again.
And now, Poke, with your consent,
I'm go' go to that-air gent
She's in love with, and confer
With *him* on his views o' *her.*—
Blast him! give the man *some* show.—
Who *is* he?—*I'm go' to know!*"
Somepin' struck the little chap
Funny, 'peared-like.—Give a slap
On his leg—laughed thue the dew
In his eyes, and says: "*It's you!*"

Yes, and—'cordin' to the last
Love-letters of ours 'at passed
Thue his hands—we was to be
Married Chris'mas.—"Gee-mun-*nee!*
Poke," says I, "it's *suddent*—yit
We *kin* make it! You're to git
Up tomorry, say, 'bout *three*—
Tell your folks you're go' with me:—
We'll hitch up, and jes drive in
'N take the town o' Chinkypin!"

GO, WINTER!

GO, Winter! Go thy ways! We want again
 The twitter of the bluebird and the wren;
Leaves ever greener growing, and the shine
    Of Summer's sun—not thine.—

Thy sun, which mocks our need of warmth and love
And all the heartening fervencies thereof,
It scarce hath heat enow to warm our thin
    Pathetic yearnings in.

So get thee from us! We are cold, God wot,
Even as *thou* art.—We remember not
How blithe we hailed thy coming.—That was O
    Too long—too long ago!

Get from us utterly! Ho! Summer then
Shall spread her grasses where thy snows have been,
And thy last icy footprint melt and mold
    In her first marigold.

ELIZABETH.

May 1, 1891.

I.

ELIZABETH! Elizabeth!
    The first May-morning whispereth
Thy gentle name in every breeze
That lispeth through the young-leaved trees,
New raimented in white and green
Of bloom and leaf to crown thee queen;—
And, as in odorous chorus, all
The orchard-blossoms sweetly call
Even as a singing voice that saith
        Elizabeth!   Elizabeth!

II.

Elizabeth!   Lo, lily-fair,
In deep, cool shadows of thy hair,
Thy face maintaineth its repose.—
Is it, O sister of the rose,
So better, sweeter, blooming thus
Than in this briery world with us?—
    Where frost o'ertaketh, and the breath
    Of biting winter harrieth
With sleeted rains and blighting snows
        All fairest blooms—Elizabeth!

III.

Nay, then!—So reign, Elizabeth,
Crowned, in thy May-day realm of death!
Put forth the scepter of thy love
In every star-tipped blossom of
The grassy dais of thy throne!
Sadder are we, thus left alone,
But gladder they that thrill to see
Thy mother's rapture, greeting thee.
   Bereaved are we by life —not death—
      Elizabeth! Elizabeth!

SLEEP.

ORPHANED, I cry to thee:
    Sweet sleep! O kneel and be
A mother unto me!
  Calm thou my childish fears:
Fold—fold mine eyelids to, all tenderly,
      And dry my tears.

Come, Sleep, all drowsy-eyed
And faint with languor,—slide
Thy dim face down beside
  Mine own, and let me rest
And nestle in thy heart, and there abide,
      A favored guest.

Good night to every care,
And shadow of despair!
Good night to all things where
  Within is no delight!—
Sleep opens her dark arms, and, swooning
    there,
      I sob: Good night—good night!

DAN PAINE.

OLD friend of mine, whose chiming name
 Has been the burthen of a rhyme
Within my heart since first I came
 To know thee in thy mellow prime:
  With warm emotions in my breast
  That can but coldly be expressed,
  And hopes and wishes wild and vain,
  I reach my hand to thee, Dan Paine.

In fancy, as I sit alone
 In gloomy fellowship with care,
I hear again thy cheery tone,
 And wheel for thee an easy chair;
  And from my hand the pencil falls—
  My book upon the carpet sprawls,
  As eager soul and heart and brain,
  Leap up to welcome thee, Dan Paine.

A something gentle in thy mein,
 A something tender in thy voice,
Has made my trouble so serene,
 I can but weep, from very choice.
  And even then my tears, I guess,
  Hold more of sweet than bitterness,
  And more of gleaming shine than rain,
  Because of thy bright smile Dan Paine.

The wrinkles that the years have spun
　And tangled round thy tawny face,
Are kinked with laughter, every one,
　And fashioned in a mirthful grace.
　　And though the twinkle of thine eyes
　　Is keen as frost when Summer dies,
　　It can not long as frost remain
　　While thy warm soul shines out, Dan Paine.

And so I drain a health to thee :—
　May merry Joy and jolly Mirth
Like children clamber on thy knee,
　And ride thee round the happy earth!
　　And when, at last, the hand of Fate
　　Shall lift the latch of Canaan's gate,
　　And usher me in thy domain,
　　Smile on me just as now, Dan Paine.

OLD WINTERS ON THE FARM

I HAVE jest about decided
    It 'ud keep a *town-boy* hoppin'
    Fer to work all winter, choppin'
Fer a' old fire-place, like *I* did!
Lawz! them old times wuz contrairy!—
    Blame backbone o' winter, 'peared-like,
    Wouldn't break! —and I wuz skeerd-like
Clean on into *February*!
    Nothin' ever made we madder
Than fer Pap to stomp in, layin'
On a' extra fore-stick, sayin'
    "Groun'hog's out and seed his shadder!"

AT UTTER LOAF.

I.

A N afternoon as ripe with heat
       As might the golden pippin be
With mellowness if at my feet
    It dropped now from the apple-tree
    My hammock swings in lazily.

II.

The boughs about me spread a shade
    That shields me from the sun, but weaves
    With breezy shuttles through the leaves
Blue rifts of skies, to gleam and fade
    Upon the eyes that only see
    Just of themselves, all drowsily.

III.

Above me drifts the fallen skein
    Of some tired spider, looped and blown,
As fragile as a strand of rain,
    Across the air, and upward thrown
    By breaths of hayfields newly mown—
So glimmering it is and fine,
I doubt these drowsy eyes of mine.

IV.

Far-off and faint as voices pent
  In mines, and heard from underground,
Come murmurs as of discontent,
  And clamorings of sullen sound
The city sends me, as, I guess,
To vex me, though they do but bless
Me in my drowsy fastnesses.

V.

I have no care. I only know
  My hammock hides and holds me here
  In lands of shade a prisoner:
While lazily the breezes blow
  Light leaves of sunshine over me,
And back and forth and to and fro
  I swing, enwrapped in some hushed glee,
  Smiling at all things drowsily.

A LOUNGER.

HE leant against a lamp-post, lost
    In some mysterious reverie:
His head was bowed; his arms were crossed;
    He yawned, and glanced evasively:
Uncrossed his arms, and slowly put
    Them back again, and scratched his side—
Shifted his weight from foot to foot,
    And gazed out no-ward, idle-eyed.

Grotesque of form and face and dress,
    And picturesque in every way—
    A figure that from day to day
Drooped with a limper laziness;
    A figure such as artists lean,
    In pictures where distress is seen,
Against low hovels where we guess
    No happiness has ever been.

A SONG OF LONG AGO.

A SONG of Long Ago:
 Sing it lightly—sing it low—
Sing it softly—like the lisping of the lips we
  used to know
When our baby-laughter spilled
From the glad hearts ever filled
With music blithe as robin ever trilled!

Let the fragrant summer-breeze,
And the leaves of locust-trees,
And the apple-buds and blossoms, and the
  wings of honey-bees,
All palpitate with glee,
Till the happy harmony
Brings back each childish joy to you and me.

Let the eyes of fancy turn
Where the tumbled pippins burn
Like embers in the orchard's lap of tangled
  grass and fern,—
There let the old path wind
In and out and on behind
The cider-press that chuckles as we grind.

Blend in the song the moan
Of the dove that grieves alone,
And the wild whir of the locust, and the
        bumble's drowsy drone ;
And the low of cows that call
Through the pasture-bars when all
The landscape fades away at evenfall.

Then, far away and clear,
Through the dusky atmosphere,
Let the wailing of the kildee be the only
        sound we hear :
O sad and sweet and low
As the memory may know
Is the glad-pathetic song of Long Ago!

THE CHANT OF THE CROSS-BEARING CHILD.

I BEAR dis cross dis many a mile.
    O de cross-bearin' chile—
        De cross-bearin' chile!

I bear dis cross 'long many a road
Wha' de pink ain't bloom' an' de grass done mowed.
    O de cross-bearin' chile—
        De cross-bearin' chile!

Hits on my conscience all dese days
Fo' ter bear de cross ut de good Lord lays
On my po' soul, an' ter lif' my praise.
    O de cross-bearin' chile—
        De cross-bearin' chile!

I 's nigh-'bout weak ez I mos' kin be,
Yit de Marstah call an' He say,—"You 's free
Fo' ter 'cept dis cross, an' ter cringe yo' knee
To no n'er man in de worl' but me!"
    O de cross-bearin' chile—
        De cross-bearin' chile!

Says you guess wrong, ef I let you guess—
Says you 'spec' mo', an'-a you git less:—
Says you go eas', says you go wes',
An' whense you fine de road ut you like bes'
You betteh take ch'ice er any er de res'!
　　　　O de cross-bearin' chile—
　　　　　　De cross-bearin' chile!

He build my feet, an' He fix de signs
Dat de shoe hit pinch an' de shoe hit bines
Ef I on'y w'ah eights an-a wanter w'ah nines;
I hone fo' de rain, an' de sun hit shines,
An' whilse I hunt de sun, hits de rain I fines.—
O-a trim my lamp, an-a gyrd my lines!
　　　　O de cross-bearin' chile—
　　　　　　De cross-bearin' chile!

I wade de wet, an' I walk de dry:
I done tromp long, an' I done clim high;
An' I pilgrim on ter de jasper sky,
An' I taken de resk fo' ter cas' my eye
Wha' de Gate swing wide an' de Lord draw nigh,
An' de Trump hit blow, an' I hear de cry,—
"You lay dat cross down by an' by!—
　　　　O de Cross-bearin' Chile—
　　　　　　De Cross-bearin' Chile!"

THANKSGIVING.

L ET us be thankful—not only because
    Since last our universal thanks were told
We have grown greater in the world's applause,
    And fortune's newer smiles surpass the old—

But thankful for all things that come as alms
    From out the open hand of Providence:—
The winter clouds and storms—the summer calms —
    The sleepless dread—the drowse of indolence.

Let us be thankful—thankful for the prayers
    Whose gracious answers were long, long delayed,
That they might fall upon us unawares,
    And bless us, as in greater need, we prayed.

Let us be thankful for the loyal hand
    That love held out in welcome to our own,
When love and *only* love could understand
    The need of touches we had never known.

Let us be thankful for the longing eyes
    That gave their secret to us as they wept,
Yet in return found, with a sweet surprise,
    Love's touch upon their lids, and, smiling, slept.

And let us, too, be thankful that the tears
　Of sorrow have not all been drained away,
That through them still, for all the coming years,
　We may look on the dead face of To-day.

AUTUMN.

A S a harvester, at dusk,
   Faring down some woody trail
Leading homeward through the musk
Of may-apple and pawpaw,
Hazel-bush, and spice and haw,—
So comes Autumn, swart and hale,
Drooped of frame and slow of stride,
But withal an air of pride
Looming up in stature far
Higher than his shoulders are;
Weary both in arm and limb,
Yet the wholesome heart of him
Sheer at rest and satisfied.

Greet him as with glee of drums
And glad cymbals, as he comes!
Robe him fair, O Rain and Shine.
He the Emperor—the King—
Royal lord of everything
Sagging Plenty's granary floors
And out-bulging all her doors;
He the god of corn and wine,
Honey, milk, and fruit and oil—
Lord of feast, as lord of toil—
Jocund host of yours and mine!

Ho! the revel of his laugh!—
Half is sound of winds, and half
Roar of ruddy blazes drawn
Up the throats of chimneys wide,
Circling which, from side to side,
Faces—lit as by the Dawn,
With her highest tintings on
Tip of nose, and cheek, and chin—
Smile at some old fairy-tale
Of enchanted lovers, in
Silken gown and coat of mail,
With a retinue of elves
Merry as their very selves,
Trooping ever, hand in hand,
Down the dales of Wonderland.

Then the glory of his song!—
Lifting up his dreamy eyes—
Singing haze across the skies;
Singing clouds that trail along
Towering tops of trees that seize
Tufts of them to stanch the breeze;
Singing slanted strands of rain
In between the sky and earth,
For the lyre to mate the mirth

And the might of his refrain:
Singing southward-flying birds
Down to us, and afterwards
Singing them to flight again;
Singing blushes to the cheeks
Of the leaves upon the trees—
Singing on and changing these
Into pallor, slowly wrought,
Till the little, moaning creeks
Bear them to their last farewell,
As Elaine, the lovable,
Was borne down to Lancelot.—
Singing drip of tears, and then
Drying them with smiles again.

Singing apple, peach and grape,
Into roundest, plumpest shape;
Rosy ripeness to the face
Of the pippin; and the grace
Of the dainty stamin-tip
To the huge bulk of the pear,
Pendant in the green caress
Of the leaves, and glowing through
With the tawny laziness
Of the gold that Ophir knew,—
Haply, too, within its rind
Such a cleft as bees may find,

Bungling on it half aware,
And wherein to see them sip
Fancy lifts an oozy lip,
And the singer's falter there.

Sweet as swallows swimming through
Eddyings of dusk and dew,
Singing happy scenes of home
Back to sight of eager eyes
That have longed for them to come,
Till their coming is surprise
Uttered only by the rush
Of quick tears and prayerful hush:
Singing on, in clearer key,
Hearty palms of you and me
Into grasps that tingle still
Rapturous, and ever will!
Singing twank and twang of strings—
Trill of flute and clarinet
In a melody that rings
Like the tunes we used to play,
And our dreams are playing yet!
Singing lovers, long astray,
Each to each; and, sweeter things,—
Singing in their marriage-day,
And a banquet holding all
These delights for festival.

THE TWINS.

ONE 'S the pictur' of his Pa,
    And the *other* of her Ma—
Jes the bossest pair o' babies 'at a mortal
      ever saw!
And we love 'em as the bees
Loves the blossoms of the trees,
A-ridin' and a-rompin' in the breeze!

One's got her Mammy's eyes—
Soft and blue as Apurl-skies—
With the same sort of a *smile*, like—Yes, and
      mouth about her size,—
Dimples, too, in cheek and chin,
'At my lips jes *wallers* in,
A-goin' to work, er gittin' home agin.

And the *other*—Well, they say
That he's got his Daddy's way
O' bein' ruther soberfied, er ruther extry gay,—
That he either cries his best,
Er he laughs his howlin'est—
Like all he lacked was buttons and a vest!

Look at *her!*—and look at *him!*—
Talk about yer " Cheru-*bim!* "
Roll 'em up in dreams together, rosy arm
    and chubby limb!
O we love 'em as the bees
Loves the blossoms of the trees,
A ridin' and a‑rompin' in the breeze!

BEDOUIN.

O LOVE is like an untamed steed!—
   So hot of heart and wild of speed,
And with fierce freedom so in love,
The desert is not vast enough,
With all its leagues of glimmering sands,
To pasture it! Ah, that my hands
Were more than human in their strength,
That my deft lariat at length
Might safely noose this splendid thing
That so defies all conquering!
Ho! but to see it whirl and reel!—
The sands spurt forward—and to feel
The quivering tension of the thong
That throned me high, with shriek and song!
To grapple tufts of tossing mane—
To spurn it to its feet again,
And then, sans saddle, rein or bit,
To lash the mad life out of it!

TUGG MARTIN.

I.

TUGG Martin's tough.—No doubt o' that!
  And down there at
The town he come from word's bin sent
Advisin' this-here Settle-ment
  To kindo' *humor* Tugg, and not
        To git him hot.—
Jest pass his imperfections by,
And he's as good as pie!

II.

They claim he's *wanted* back there.—Yit
The officers they mostly quit
        Insistin' when
They notice Tugg's so *back'ard*, and
Sorto' gives 'em to understand
  He druther not!—A Deputy
  (The slickest one you ever see!)
Tackled him *last*—"disguisin' then,"
As Tugg says, "as *a gentlemen!*"—
  You'd ort o' hear *Tugg* tell it!—*My!*
        I thought I'd *die!*

III.

The way it wuz:—Tugg and the rest
    The boys wuz jest
A-kindo' gittin' thawed out, down
At "Guss's Place," fur-end o' town,
  One night, when, first we knowed,
      Some feller rode
Up in a buggy at the door,
  And hollered fer some one to come
      And fetch him some
Red-licker out—And whirped and swore
That colt he drove wuz " *Thompson's* " shore!

IV.

Guss went out, and come in agin
  And filled a pint and tuck it out—
Stayed quite a spell—then peeked back in,
  Half-hid-like where the light wuz dim,
      And jieuked his head
      At Tugg and said,—
" Come out a minute—here's a gent
  Wants you to take a drink with him."

V.

Well—Tugg laid down his cards and went—
        In fact, *we all*
                Got up, you know,
                Startin' to go—
When in reels Guss aginst the wall,
                As white as snow,
Gaspin',—"*He's tuck Tugg!—Wher's my gun?*"
    And-sir, outside we heerd
The hoss snort and kick up his heels
    Like he wuz skeerd,
And then the buggy-wheels
Scrape—and then *Tugg's* voice hollerun',—
    "*I'm bested!—Good-bye, fellers!*" . . . 'Peared
                S' all-fired suddent,
                Nobody couldn't
Jest git it fixed,—tel hoss and man,
    Buggy and Tugg, off through the dark
Went like the devil beatin' tan-
                Bark !

VI.

What *could* we do? . . . We filed back to
    The bar: And Guss jest *looked* at us,
And we looked back "The same as you,"

Still *sayin'* nothin'—And the sap
   It stood in every eye,
And every hat and cap
Went off, as we teched glasses solemnly,
   And Guss says-he:
"Ef it's 'good-bye' with Tugg, fer *shore*,—I say
  God bless him!—Er ef they
  Aint railly no *need* to pray,
I'm not *reniggin'*—board's the play,
And here's God bless him, anyway!"

VII.

It must a-bin an hour er so
   We all set there,
 Talkin o' pore
   Old Tugg, you know,
'At never wuz ketched up before—
When—all slow-like—the door-
Knob turned—and Tugg come shamblin' in,
 Hand-cuffed!—'at's what he wuz, I swear!—
   Yit smilin,' like he hadn't bin
 Away at all! And when we ast him where
The *Deputy* wuz at,—"I don't know *where*," Tugg
  said,—
   "All *I* know is—he's dead."

LET US FORGET.

L ET us forget. What matters it that we
    Once reigned o'er happy realms of long-ago,
  And talked of love, and let our voices low,
And ruled for some brief sessions royally?
What if we sung, or laughed, or wept maybe?
  It has availed not anything, and so
  Let it go by that we may better know
How poor a thing is lost to you and me.
  But yesterday I kissed your lips, and yet
Did thrill you not enough to shake the dew
    From your drenched lids—and missed, with no
        regret,
Your kiss shot back, with sharp breaths failing you:
  And so, to-day, while our worn eyes are wet
  With all this waste of tears, let us forget!

JOHN ALDEN AND PERCILLY.

W E got up a Christmas-doin's
　　Last Christmas Eve—
Kindo' dimonstration
　'At I railly believe
Give more satisfaction—
　　Take it up and down—
Than ary intertainment
　　Ever come to town!

Railly was a *theater*—
　　That's what it was,—
But, bein' in the church, you know,
　　We had a *"Santy Clause"*—
So's to git the *old folks*
　　To patternize, you see,
And *back* the institootion up
　　Kindo' *morally.*

Schoolteacher writ the thing—
　　(Was a friend o' mine),
Got it out o' Longfeller's
　　Pome "Evangeline"—
Er some'rs—'bout the *Purituns*—.
　　*Any*way, the part
"*John Alden*" fell to *me*—
　　And learnt it all by heart!

Claircy was "*Percilly*"—
　(Schoolteacher 'lowed
Me and her could act them two
　Best of all the crowd)—
Then—blame ef he didn't
　Git her Pap, i jing!—
To take the part o' "*Santy Clause,*"
　To wind up the thing.

Law! the fun o' practisun!—
　Was a week er two
Me and Claircy didn't have
　Nothin' else to do!—
Kep' us jes a-meetin' round,
　Kindo' here and there,
Ever' night rehearsin'-like,
　And gaddin' ever'where!

Game was wo'th the candle, though!—
　Christmas Eve at last
Rolled around.—And 'tendance jes
　Couldn't been su'passed!—
Neighbors from the country
　Come from Clay and Rush—
Yes, and 'crost the county-line
　Clean from Puckerbrush!

Meetin'-house jes trimbled
　　As "Old Santy" went
Round amongst the childern,
　　With their pepperment
And sassafrac and wintergreen
　　Candy, and " a ball
O' popcorn," the preacher 'nounced,
　　"Free fer each and all! "

Schoolteacher suddently
　　Whispered in my ear,—
"Guess I got you:—*Christmas-gift !—*
　　Christmas is here !"
I give *him* a gold pen,
　　And case to hold the thing.—
And *Claircy* whispered *"Christmas-gift!"*
　　And I give her *a ring.*

"And now," says I, "jes watch *me*—
　　Christmas-gift," says i,
"*I'm* a-goin' to git one—
　　'*Santy's*' comin' by!"—
Then I rech and grabbed him:
　　And, as you 'll infer,
'Course I got the old man's,
　　And *he* gimme *her!*

REACH YOUR HAND TO ME.

REACH your hand to me, my friend,
  With its heartiest caress—
Sometime there will come an end
  To its present faithfulness—
      Sometime I may ask in vain
      For the touch of it again,
      When between us land or sea
      Holds it ever back from me.

Sometime I may need it so,
  Groping somewhere in the night,
It will seem to me as though
  Just a touch, however light,
      Would make all the darkness day,
      And along some sunny way
      Lead me through an April-shower
      Of my tears to this fair hour.

O the present is too sweet
  To go on forever thus!
Round the corner of the street
  Who can say what waits for us?—
      Meeting—greeting, night and day,
      Faring each the self-same way—
      Still somewhere the path must end.—
      Reach your hand to me, my friend!

THE ROSE.

IT tossed its head at the wooing breeze;
　And the sun, like a bashful swain,
Beamed on it through the waving trees
　With a passion all in vain,—
For my rose laughed in a crimson glee,
And hid in the leaves in wait for me.

The honey-bee came there to sing
　His love through the languid hours,
And vaunt of his hives, as a proud old king
　Might boast of his palace-towers:
But my rose bowed in a mockery,
And hid in the leaves in wait for me.

The humming-bird, like a courtier gay,
　Dipped down with a dalliant song,
And twanged his wings through the roundelay
　Of love the whole day long:
Yet my rose turned from his minstrelsy
And hid in the leaves in wait for me.

The firefly came in the twilight dim
  My red, red rose to woo—
Till quenched was the flame of love in him,
  And the light of his lantern too,
As my rose wept with dewdrops three
And hid in the leaves in wait for me.

And I said: I will cull my own sweet rose—
  Some day I will claim as mine
The priceless worth of the flower that knows
  No change, but a bloom divine—
The bloom of a fadeless constancy
That hides in the leaves in wait for me!

But time passed by in a strange disguise,
  And I marked it not, but lay
In a lazy dream, with drowsy eyes,
  Till the summer slipped away,
And a chill wind sang in a minor key:
"Where is the rose that waits for thee?"

        *   *   *   *   *   *   *   *

I dream to-day, o'er a purple stain
  Of bloom on a withered stalk,
Pelted down by the autumn rain
  In the dust of the garden-walk,
That an Angel-rose in the world to be
Will hide in the leaves in wait for me.

MY FRIEND.

"HE is my friend," I said,—
"Be patient!" Overhead
The skies were drear and dim;
And lo! the thought of him
Smiled on my heart—and then
The sun shone out again!

"He is my friend!" The words
Brought summer and the birds;
And all my winter-time
Thawed into running rhyme
And rippled into song,
Warm, tender, brave, and strong.

And so it sings to-day.—
So may it sing alway!
Though waving grasses grow
Between, and lilies blow
Their trills of perfume clear
As laughter to the ear,
Let each mute measure end
With "Still he is thy friend."

SUSPENSE.

A WOMAN'S figure, on a ground of night
  Inlaid with sallow stars that dimly stare
Down in the lonesome eyes, uplifted there
As in vague hope some alien lance of light
Might pierce their woe. The tears that blind her sight—
  The salt and bitter blood of her despair—
  Her hands toss back through torrents of her hair
And grip toward God with anguish infinite.
  And O the carven mouth, with all its great
Intensity of longing frozen fast
  In such a smile as well may designate
The slowly-murdered heart, that, to the last,
  Conceals each newer wound, and back at Fate
Throbs Love's eternal lie—"Lo, I can wait!"

THE PASSING OF A HEART.

O TOUCH me with your hands—
                   For pity's sake!
My brow throbs ever on with such an ache
As only your cool touch may take away;
And so, I pray
         You, touch me with your hands!

Touch—touch me with your hands.—
                 Smooth back the hair
You once caressed, and kissed, and called so fair
That I did dream its gold would wear alway,
And lo, to-day—
         O touch me with your hands!

Just touch me with your hands,
               And let them press
My weary eyelids with the old caress,
And lull me till I sleep. Then go your way,
That Death may say:
         He touched her with his hands.

BY HER WHITE BED.

B Y her white bed I muse a little space:
     She fell asleep—not very long ago,—
And yet the grass was here and not the snow—
The leaf, the bud, the blossom, and—her face!—
Midsummer's heaven above us, and the grace
Of Love's own day, from dawn to afterglow;
The fireflies' glimmering, and the sweet and low
Plaint of the whip-poor-wills, and every place
In thicker twilight for the roses' scent.
Then *night*.—She slept—in such tranquility,
I walk atiptoe still, nor *dare* to weep,
Feeling, in all this hush, she rests content—
That though God stood to wake her for me, she
Would mutely plead: "Nay, Lord! Let *him* so
    sleep."

WE TO SIGH INSTEAD OF SING.

" RAIN and rain! and rain and rain!"
     Yesterday we muttered
Grimly as the grim refrain
     That the thunders uttered:
All the heavens under cloud—
     All the sunshine sleeping;
All the grasses limply bowed
     With their weight of weeping.

Sigh and sigh! and sigh and sigh!
     Never end of sighing;
Rain and rain for our reply—
     Hopes half-drowned and dying;
Peering through the window-pane,
     Naught but endless raining—
Endless sighing, and, as vain,
     Endlessly complaining.

Shine and shine! and shine and shine!
     Ah! to-day the splendor!—
All this glory yours and mine—
     God! but God is tender!
We to sigh instead of sing,
     Yesterday, in sorrow,
While the Lord was fashioning
     This for our To-morrow!

THE BLOSSOMS ON THE TREES.

BLOSSOMS crimson, white, or blue,
  Purple, pink, and every hue,
From sunny skies, to tintings drowned
  In dusky drops of dew,
I praise you all, wherever found,
  And love you through and through;—
    But, Blossoms On The Trees,
      With your breath upon the breeze,
There's nothing all the world around
  As half as sweet as you!

Could the rhymer only wring
  All the sweetness to the lees
Of all the kisses clustering
  In juicy Used-to-bes,
To dip his rhymes therein and sing
  The blossoms on the trees,—
"O Blossoms on the Trees,"
  He would twitter, trill and coo,
"However sweet, such songs as these
  Are not as sweet as you:—
For you are *blooming* melodies
  The *eyes* may listen to!"

A DISCOURAGING MODEL.

JUST the airiest, fairiest slip of a thing,
  With a Gainsborough hat, like a butterfly's wing,
Tilted up at one side with the jauntiest air,
And a knot of red roses sown in under there
    Where the shadows are lost in her hair.

Then a cameo face, carven in on a ground
Of that shadowy hair where the roses are wound;
And the gleam of a smile O as fair and as faint
And as sweet as the masters of old used to paint
    Round the lips of their favorite saint!

And that lace at her throat—and the fluttering hands
Snowing there, with a grace that no art understands,
The flakes of their touches—first fluttering at
The bow—then the roses—the hair—and then that
    Little tilt of the Gainsborough hat.

O what artist on earth with a model like this,
Holding not on his palette the tint of a kiss,
Nor a pigment to hint of the hue of her hair,
Nor the gold of her smile—O what artist could dare
    To expect a result half so fair?

LAST NIGHT—AND THIS.

L AST night—how deep the darkness was!
  And well I knew its depths, because
I waded it from shore to shore,
Thinking to reach the light no more.

She would not even touch my hand.—
The winds rose and the cedars fanned
The moon out, and the stars fled back
In heaven and hid—and all was black!

But ah! To-night a summons came,
Signed with a teardrop for a name,—
For as I wondering kissed it, lo,
A line beneath it told me so.

And *now*—the moon hangs over me
A disk of dazzling brilliancy,
And every star-tip stabs my sight
With splintered glitterings of light!

SEPTEMBER DARK.

I.

THE air falls chill;
   The whip-poor-will
Pipes lonesomely behind the hill:
The dusk grows dense,
The silence tense;
And lo, the katydids commence.

II.

Through shadowy rifts
Of woodland, lifts
The low, slow moon, and upward drifts,
While left and right
The fireflies' light
Swirls eddying in the skirts of Night.

III.

O Cloudland, gray
And level, lay
Thy mists across the face of Day!
At foot and head,
Above the dead,
O Dews, weep on uncomforted!

A GLIMPSE OF PAN.

I CAUGHT but a glimpse of him. Summer was
    here,
And I strayed from the town and its dust and heat
And walked in a wood, while the noon was near,
Where the shadows were cool, and the atmosphere
    Was misty with fragrances stirred by my feet
From surges of blossoms that billowed sheer
    O'er the grasses, green and sweet.

And I peered through a vista of leaning trees,
    Tressed with long tangles of vines that swept
To the face of a river, that answered these
With vines in the wave like the vines in the breeze,
    Till the yearning lips of the ripples crept
And kissed them, with quavering ecstacies,
    And gurgled and laughed and wept.

And there, like a dream in a swoon, I swear
    I saw Pan lying,—his limbs in the dew
And the shade, and his face in the dazzle and glare
Of the glad sunshine; while everywhere,
    Over, across, and around him blew
Filmy dragonflies hither and there,
    And little white butterflies, two and two,
        In eddies of odorous air.

OUT OF NAZARETH.

"HE shall sleep unscathed of thieves
   Who loves Allah and believes."
Thus heard one who shared the tent,
In the far-off Orient,
Of the Bedouin ben Ahrzz —
Nobler never loved the stars
Through the palm-leaves nigh the dim
Dawn his courser neighed to him!

He said: "Let the sands be swarmed
   With such thieves as I, and thou
Shalt at morning rise, unharmed,
   Light as eyelash to the brow
Of thy camel, amber-eyed,
Ever munching either side,
Striding still, with nestled knees,
Through the midnight's oases.

"Who can rob thee an thou hast
   More than this that thou hast cast
At my feet—this dust of gold?
Simply this and that, all told!
Hast thou not a treasure of
Such a thing as men call love?

"Can the dusky band I lead
  Rob thee of thy daily need
  Of a whiter soul, or steal
  What thy lordly prayers reveal?
  Who could be enriched of thee
  By such hoard of poverty
  As thy niggard hand pretends
  To dole me—thy worst of friends?
    Therefore shouldst thou pause to bless
  One indeed who blesses thee:
    Robbing thee, I dispossess
  But myself.—Pray thou for me!"

He shall sleep unscathed of thieves
Who loves Allah and believes.

THE WANDERING JEW.

THE stars are failing, and the sky
   Is like a field of faded flowers;
The winds on weary wings go by;
  The moon hides, and the temptest lowers;
     And still through every clime and age
     I wander on a pilgrimage
     That all men know an idle quest,
     For that the goal I seek is—REST!

I hear the voice of summer streams,
  And, following, I find the brink
Of cooling springs, with childish dreams
  Returning as I bend to drink—
     But suddenly, with startled eyes,
     My face looks on its grim disguise
     Of long gray beard; and so, distressed,
     I hasten on, nor taste of rest.

I come upon a merry group
  Of children in the dusky wood,
Who answer back the owlet's whoop,
  That laughs as it had understood;
     And I would pause a little space,
     But that each happy blossom-face
     Is like to one *His* hands have blessed
     Who sent me forth in search of rest.

Sometimes I fain would stay my feet
  In shady lanes, where huddled kine
Couch in the grasses cool and sweet,
  And lift their patient eyes to mine;
      But I, for thoughts that ever then
      Go back to Bethlehem again,
      Must needs fare on my weary quest,
      And weep for very need of rest.

Is there no end? I plead in vain:
  Lost worlds nor living answer me.
Since Pontius Pilate's awful reign
  Have I not passed eternity?
      Have I not drank the fetid breath
      Of every fevered phase of death,
      And come unscathed through every pest
      And scourge and plague that promised rest?

Have I not seen the stars go out
  That shed their light o'er Galilee,
And mighty kingdoms tossed about
  And crumbled clod-like in the sea?
      Dead ashes of dead ages blow
      And cover me like drifting snow,
      And time laughs on as 'twere a jest
      That I have any need of rest.

LONGFELLOW.

THE winds have talked with him confidingly;
   The trees have whispered to him; and the night
  Hath held him gently as a mother might,
And taught him all sad tones of melody:
The mountains have bowed to him; and the sea,
   In clamorous waves, and murmurs exquisite,
  Hath told him all her sorrow and delight—
Her legends fair—her darkest mystery.
  His verse blooms like a flower, night and day;
Bees cluster round his rhymes; and twitterings
  Of lark and swallow, in an endless May,
Are mingling with the tender songs he sings.—
  Nor shall he cease to sing—in every lay
  Of Nature's voice he sings—and will alway.

JOHN McKEEN.

JOHN McKEEN, in his rusty dress,
   His loosened collar, and swarthy throat;
His face unshaven, and none the less,
His hearty laugh and his wholesomeness,
   And the wealth of a workman's vote!

Bring him, O Memory, here once more,
   And tilt him back in his windsor chair
By the kitchen-stove, when the day is o'er
And the light of the hearth is across the floor,
   And the crickets everywhere!

And let their voices be gladly blent
   With a watery jingle of pans and spoons,
And a motherly chirrup of sweet content,
And neighborly gossip and merriment,
   And old-time fiddle-tunes!

Tick the clock with a wooden sound,
   And fill the hearing with childish glee
Of rhyming riddle, or story found
In the Robinson Crusoe, leather-bound
   Old book of the Used-to-be!

John McKeen of the Past!   Ah, John,
   To have grown ambitious in worldly ways!—
To have rolled your shirt-sleeves down, to don
A broadcloth suit, and, forgetful, gone
   Out on election days!

John, ah, John! did it prove your worth
   To yield you the office you still maintain?
To fill your pockets, but leave the dearth
Of all the happier things on earth
   To the hunger of heart and brain?

Under the dusk of your villa trees,
   Edging the drives where your blooded span
Paw the pebbles and wait your ease,—
Where are the children about your knees,
   And the mirth, and the happy man?

The blinds of your mansion are battened to ;
   Your faded wife is a close recluse ;
And your "finished" daughters will doubtless do
Dutifully all that is willed of you,
   And marry as you shall choose!—

But O for the old-home voices, blent
   With the watery jingle of pans and spoons,
And the motherly chirrup of glad content,
And neighborly gossip and merriment,
   And the old-time fiddle-tunes!

THEIR SWEET SORROW.

THEY meet to say farewell: Their way
    Of saying this is hard to say.—
He holds her hand an instant, wholly
Distressed—and she unclasps it slowly.

He bends *his* gaze evasively
Over the printed page that she
    Recurs to, with a new-moon shoulder
    Glimpsed from the lace-mists that enfold her.

The clock, beneath its crystal cup,
Discreetly clicks—" *Quick! Act! Speak up!* "
    A tension circles both her slender
    Wrists—and her raised eyes flash in splendor,

Even as he feels his dazzled own.—
Then, blindingly, round either thrown,
    They feel a stress of arms that ever
    Strain tremblingly—and " *Never! Never!* "

Is whispered brokenly, with half
A sob, like a belated laugh,—
    While cloyingly their blurred kiss closes,
    Sweet as the dew's lip to the rose's.

SOME SCATTERING REMARKS OF BUB'S.

WUNST I tooked our pepper-box lid
    An' cut little pie-dough biscuits, I did,
And cooked 'em on our stove one day
When our hired girl she said I may.

Honey's the goodest thing—Oo-*ooh!*
And blackberry-pies is goodest, too!
But wite hot biscuits, ist soakin'-wet
Wiv tree-mullasus, is goodest yet!

Miss Maimie she's my Ma's friend,—an'
She's purtiest girl in all the lan'!—
An' sweetest smile an' voice an' face—
An' eyes ist looks like p'serves tas'e'!

I *ruther* go to the Circus-show;
But, 'cause my *parunts* told me so,
I ruther go to the Sund'y School,
'Cause there I learn the goldun rule.

Say, Pa,—what *is* the goldun rule
'At's allus at the Sund'y School?

MR. WHAT'S-HIS-NAME.

THEY called him Mr. What's-his-name:
From where he was, or why he came,
Or when, or what he found to do,
Nobody in the city knew.

He lived, it seemed, shut up alone
In a low hovel of his own;
There cooked his meals and made his bed,
Careless of all his neighbors said.

His neighbors, too, said many things
Expressive of grave wonderings,
Since none of them had ever been
Within his doors, or peered therein.

In fact, grown watchful, they became
Assured that Mr. What's-his-name
Was up to something wrong—indeed,
Small doubt of it, we all agreed.

At night were heard strange noises there,
When honest people everywhere
Had long retired; and his light
Was often seen to burn all night.

He left his house but seldom—then
Would always hurry back again,
As though he feared some stranger's knock,
Finding him gone, might burst the lock.

Beside, he carried, every day,
At the one hour he went away,
A basket, with the contents hid
Beneath its woven willow lid.

And so we grew to greatly blame
This wary Mr. What's-his-name,
And look on him with such distrust
His actions seemed to sanction just.

But when he died—he died one day—
Dropped in the street while on his way
To that old wretched hut of his—
You'll think it strange—perhaps it is—

But when we lifted him, and past
The threshold of his home at last,
No man of all the crowd but stepped
With reverence,—Aye, *quailed* and *wept!*

What was it? Just a shriek of pain
I pray to never hear again—
A withered woman, old and bowed,
That fell and crawled and cried aloud—

And kissed the dead man's matted hair—
Lifted his face and kissed him there—
Called to him, as she clutched his hand,
In words no one could understand.

Insane? Yes.—Well, we, searching, found
An unsigned letter, in a round
Free hand, within the dead man's breast:
"Look to my mother—*I'm* at rest.

'You'l find **my** money safely hid
Under the lining of the lid
Of my work-basket. It is hers,
And God will bless her ministers!"

And some day—though he died unknown—
If through the City by the Throne
I walk, all cleansed of earthly shame,
I'll ask for Mr. What's-his-name.

WHEN AGE COMES ON.

WHEN Age comes on!—
  The deepening dusk is where the dawı
 Once glittered splendid, and the dew
In honey-drips, from red rose-lips
 Was kissed away by me and you.—
And now across the frosty lawn
Black foot-prints trail, and Age comes on—
   And Age comes on!
 And biting wild-winds whistle through
Our tattered hopes—and Age comes on!

When Age comes on!—
O tide of raptures, long withdrawn,
 Flow back in summer-floods, and fling
Here at our feet our childhood sweet,
 And all the songs we used to sing!...
Old loves, old friends—all dead and gone—
Our old faith lost—and Age comes on—
   And Age comes on!
 Poor hearts! have we not anything
But longings left when Age comes on?

ENVOY.

JUST as of old! The world rolls on and on;
    The day dies into night—night into dawn—
Dawn into dusk—through centuries untold.—
            Just as of old.

Time loiters not. The river ever flows,
Its brink or white with blossoms or with snows;
Its tide or warm with Spring or Winter cold:
            Just as of old.

Lo! where is the beginning, where the end
Of living, loving, longing? *Listen*, friend!—
God answers with a silence of pure gold—
            Just as of old.

www.ingramcontent.com/pod-product-compliance
Lightning Source LLC
Chambersburg PA
CBHW030124030726

47498CB00007B/2531